Dangerous Undertaking

Mark de Castrique

Poisoned Pen Press

Copyright © 2003 by Mark de Castrique

First Edition 2003

10 9 8 7 6 5 4 3 2 1

Library of Congress Catalog Card Number: 2003100082

ISBN: 1-590580-55-9   Hardcover

Poisoned Pen Press
6962 E. First Ave. Ste. 103
Scottsdale, AZ 85251
www.poisonedpenpress.com
info@poisonedpenpress.com

Printed in the United States of America

For Linda and our daughters Melissa and Lindsay

Acknowledgments

Thanks to the many friends whose encouragement and support made this book possible. Thanks to Robert and Barbara, their nurturing staff at Poisoned Pen Press, and my agent Linda Allen, and a special thank you to Steve Greene, whose fingerprints are on every page...admissible evidence of his conscientious service to the reader. And my father Arch whose years as a funeral director in the mountains helped bring the characters to life.

Chapter 1

Crab Apple Valley Baptist Church sat high on a grassy knoll overseeing the sinners scattered along the valley floor. A gravel road curved up to a parking lot adjacent to the simple, white-framed structure. Our hearse was already backed up close to the front door.

On the other side of the church, the cemetery sprawled down the hillside. A green canvas awning rose over a freshly dug grave and advertised the services of Clayton and Clayton Funeral Directors. We had been able to set up close to the sanctuary because Martha Willard's family had been one of the valley's first settlers and enjoyed a family plot of choice proximity.

Wayne Thompson, my uncle, waved to me as I pulled into the far corner of the gravel lot and left closer parking for the family and mourners. For such a small funeral, he had brought only one other man. There would be no family limousine or procession.

Wayne smiled from underneath the oversized black umbrella as he came over to offer me its temporary shelter while I pulled my own from the back seat.

"Everything's under control, Barry. Freddy and I have already positioned the casket in front of the altar." He stepped back as I pressed the release button and my umbrella launched into shape.

"Good. Any problem with the vault?" I asked.

"No. Rain is flowing away from the grave. The immediate family can fit under the tent and the rest of us will be under umbrellas. I threw an extra ten in the hearse."

"How's the family doing?"

"Pretty good, I guess," said Wayne. "Preacher Stinnett's been dealing with them. I gather there's a little family tension."

We began walking toward the front of the church. I kept glancing down to avoid the puddles. Wayne glided along in the precise gait bred by years of escorting the bereaved, as he watched the main road for any sign of early mourners. Uncle Wayne and my father had been burying the people of Laurel County for over forty years.

"Norma Jean's taken charge of things," he continued. "She's the one who prearranged the funeral."

That had been unusual, even if the service was for someone like Martha Willard who got so out of it toward the end. Most of the mountain people I knew were too superstitious to finalize a funeral unless death was imminent—as in before sunset.

"And the others?" I asked. "Lee and Dallas? They doing all right?"

"Lee is doing what Norma Jean and Preacher Stinnett tell him. Dallas? Well, I ain't seen him yet. Nobody's seen him. Leastwise, that's what Preacher Stinnett said earlier this morning. Norma Jean told him when Grandma Martha died, Dallas walked out of the room without saying a word. At first they were mad, then after two days passed, they got worried. I think they're afraid he might have hurt himself. Lee and the preacher stopped by his cabin at seven this morning, but he wasn't there."

"I was afraid he'd take her death awfully hard."

"Yeah,' said Uncle Wayne. "Well, Dallas is a strange one, that's for sure."

We spent the next forty-five minutes arranging flowers, placing folding chairs at the graveside, and setting up the

"Those Who Called" book in the vestibule for attendees to sign. About quarter to ten, people began to arrive. I worked in the parking lot, passing out umbrellas and directing traffic.

At ten o'clock, Wayne joined me. He scanned the valley, and the irritation broke through his voice. "I got the family all settled in the front pew, but no one has seen hide nor hair of Dallas." He checked his watch. "I hate a third of the family ain't here, but I'm giving Preacher Stinnett the signal in ten minutes whether Dallas has the decency to show up or not. You may as well go on in."

Inside the narrow sanctuary, mourners sat in scattered clumps along the hand-hewn pews. Necks twisted around as my footsteps echoed on the wide-plank pine floor. I felt like a bride at the wrong wedding, and I made a hasty retreat off to the side. People continued to look toward the rear of the church making me realize they were awaiting the arrival of Dallas Willard. Many faces were familiar enough to have names attached. Others belonged to the nameless folks you cross paths with in a small community, seeing each other at the Post Office or Farmer's Market.

Across the aisle sat a man who seemed out of place with the simpler mountain folk. The tailored cut of his dark suit spoke of power, and the perfectly trimmed steel-gray hair and robust tan reeked money. I couldn't place him though he looked at me and nodded a silent greeting. Then he glanced behind me to the door. I turned and saw Wayne give a single distinct nod to Preacher Stinnett.

The scripture was read in predictable order: a few passages of Psalms followed by New Testament assurances of Everlasting Life. Preacher Stinnett kept his eulogy brief, emphasizing Martha Willard's good works and her love for her family. I suspected he wanted to get everyone out to the grave and back before the heavens opened up. He walked to the closed casket in front of the altar and gave a prayer for Martha's soul with a plea that all would know Jesus like Martha now did.

At the "Amen," our assistant, Freddy Mott, motioned for the pallbearers to stand. Then the congregation rose as Martha left the church for the final time.

We led the procession down the steps and around to the cemetery. The weather had thickened. Umbrellas sprang up in the dampness like mushrooms. A British novel of forgotten title came to mind because it was the first time I had read the word mizzle—to rain so fine that the droplets hung in the air without falling to earth. Mist and drizzle merged to mizzle. The effect was "mizzlerable."

Norma Jean and Lee joined Preacher Stinnett and the casket under the tent. The rest of us encircled them, the men giving way for the women and a few children to stand under the protection of the canvas. I wound up just behind the family, positioned beside a frail, thin tombstone, trying to keep the water on my umbrella from draining down the necks of my neighbors.

Preacher Stinnett cleared his throat, and then stopped short of speaking. Through the silence came the steady crunch of gravel from the footsteps of a latecomer. All heads turned toward the approaching sound.

Dallas Willard, lips drawn tight across his expressionless face, strode stiff-legged out of the mist, his head uncovered, his body shrouded in a long gray coat that brushed the ground, and his hands buried in his pockets. He materialized like some Civil War soldier snatched from a Mathew Brady photograph. I wouldn't have been surprised if a ghostly cavalry horse had trailed him.

People parted to let him get to the casket. Dallas walked through them like they didn't exist. He stopped at the foot, not crossing over to stand beside his brother and sister. He neither looked at them nor at Preacher Stinnett. Instead, his gaze fell upon only one person. His gaze fell upon me.

I nodded but said nothing. His hair looked like wet straw. Rivulets ran down his cheeks, but I couldn't tell whether they were tears or simply condensed moisture. Then his thin lips broke into a smile of some shared secret that set my neck tingling.

"And now that we are all finally gathered here," lectured Preacher Stinnett, "let us bow our heads, close our eyes, and pray together the prayer our Lord taught us."

Reluctantly, I looked down, sensing that Dallas still stared at me.

"Thy Kingdom come" was followed by the ear-splitting blast of a shotgun. I snapped my eyes open to see Lee Willard hurled back against a tombstone. Dallas stood with the great coat open and the twelve-gauge level at his waist. Before anyone could take a breath, he pumped the action and kicked the spent shell onto Martha's casket. Norma Jean tried to turn away, but the second blast caught her in the side, and I heard the sickening gasp as the life-breath was wrenched from her lungs. Again, Dallas reloaded, but this time he swung the gun at me. Steam boiled off the hot barrel.

"They're goin' to Hell," he shouted. "And so am I. Tell Grandma I'll save the land. Tell her I love her."

Even before he began speaking, somehow the muddled gray cells of my brain realized Dallas Willard meant to kill me. In that split-second, I reacted. I threw the open umbrella at him as I flung myself toward the protection of the tombstone.

The buckshot blasted through the flying umbrella as if it were tissue paper. The pellets hit my left shoulder with such force that the impact twisted my mid-air flight and sent me crashing on my face lengthwise behind the grave marker. Pain seared down my arm and I couldn't move.

Dallas fired again and the century-old tombstone disintegrated above my head. Dust and granite chips rained down on me. Somewhere, a woman screamed. I rolled over on my back and clutched my shoulder. The warm, sticky dampness spread between my fingers. I opened my eyes and saw only the thick gray sky.

Time passed in a blur of detached images. Preacher Stinnett's face obliterated the sky as he knelt over me, trying to save my soul. I heard myself shout for Uncle Wayne which must have been alarming—a wounded, bleeding man calling for an undertaker. Wayne was the only person I knew skilled in first aid. Others rushed around me amid a continuous chorus of screams and moans. Hysteria predominated.

Suddenly, he was there, pulling my hand away from the wound. "Winged you," Uncle Wayne said, and smiled with reassurance. "No artery damage, but your Sunday-go-to-meeting suit is a goner."

I squeezed his arm and let him know I was okay. "The others?" I asked.

"Norma Jean and Lee are dead. Dallas got away in his pickup. It's a miracle none of the bystanders were hit. I guess the buckshot never spread out enough." Wayne looked up and yelled, "Freddy, get the hearse up here. Make sure someone phones the sheriff. And tell the hospital we're coming in." He turned back to me. "You don't mind going by hearse, do you?"

"As long as it doesn't become a habit."

A few minutes later, I was lifted into the back of the long black vehicle. The floor was not padded, but then the regular passengers rarely complained. Several of the men shed their raincoats and tucked them under me. I felt a weariness wash over me, and my arm and shoulder began to throb. I closed my eyes. Sounds collapsed into a muffled roar as I tumbled down a long well into darkness.

Chapter 2

I opened my eyes to a small, dim, private hospital room. The institutional clock by the wall-mounted television read six P.M. My stay in the recovery room must have been textbook timing.

I tried to move and felt the bandages crossing my chest. My right arm was free, but the left was bound tightly to my side. A mound of dressing covered my shoulder and arm down to the elbow. My left hand rested on my stomach, and with cautious concentration, I wiggled each finger. Everything seemed to be in working order.

My mouth was so dry I thought my tongue was welded to the roof. Post-anesthetized cotton mouth makes swallowing a Herculean effort and chips of ice more precious than diamonds. I wanted a few slivers to melt down my throat and would have sold everything I owned to get them.

A service cart was adjacent to the right side of the bed, and on it sat a white Styrofoam water pitcher. The Holy Grail could not have been more desirable. I searched for a cup, but the nurse's aide had forgotten to leave one. She had also forgotten to put the call button by my good arm, and no amount of stretching could bring it within reach.

Where there is a will, there is a way; and I figured water straight from the pitcher was better than no water at all. As I lifted it to me, the weight didn't feel like water. Sure enough, only ice was inside. The aide must have left it just moments before I awoke. No melting had occurred.

I tipped the pitcher against my lips, thrusting my tongue out to snare this frozen manna from heaven. Nothing. The ice remained fused in the bottom half. I banged the rim against my teeth, hoping to shake loose a few crystals. Instead, the confined snowstorm broke loose, and the entire contents crashed into my face and tumbled down my neck and under the flimsy hospital gown. My "god-dammit" was followed by the sound of unrestrained laughter. I brushed the ice from my eyes and saw the blurry silhouette of a woman standing in the doorway.

"Well, if you nurses had any brains, you would have put the damn button within reach."

The laughter abruptly halted.

Her voice took on the tone of one used to being obeyed. "And how many times do I have to tell you the nurses in this understaffed and underfunded hospital work their tails off? As for me, I didn't have the brains to be a nurse. I had to settle for being a surgeon who carves up undertakers that are so foolish they let their clients shoot them."

She marched over, bent down, and kissed me on the lips. Without another word, she began picking up the clumps of ice now melting through the sheets and gown. The chill had cleared my head enough to appreciate her delicate hands. I shifted my attention to her long neck and mahogany-colored hair. Dark brown eyes and pursed full lips gave evidence of the concentration and concern she brought to her work.

"Okay, Susan, you already know I'm a jerk. I had just hoped to keep you from discovering how big a jerk I am. I can only plead that I don't get shot everyday."

She smiled. "I don't often see my patients try to freeze themselves, and I don't operate on my boyfriend everyday."

"I thought it was policy not to operate on loved ones?"

"Then next time I'll just let you bleed till Dr. O'Malley drives back from Myrtle Beach. I suppose now you're going to weasel out of our Friday night date."

"Of course not. How big is this bed?"

She didn't laugh at my joke. "Not nearly as big as your male ego. You're going to be out of action for a while, Barry. That was a close call. You almost wound up in your own funeral home."

Her words sobered me. "Tell me how it went. What's the prognosis for patient Barry Clayton?"

"Good," she said. "Mostly because of luck, not my skills. The mass of pellets missed you. The anesthesiologist shoots ducks and figures from the size of the pellets they were number one buck with about twenty in the shell. Only six struck your shoulder and upper arm. They hit head on and lodged in the joint space. We had to extract them and re-tie some of the muscles in the most traumatized area."

"Movement restricted?" I asked.

"You'll have reduced latitude. Sort of like you had a chronic dislocation problem only the damage wasn't done by the bone popping out. It was the pellets tearing their way in. You'll need six weeks for healing along with simple physical therapy to stretch the muscles we had to shorten. The shoulder will be sore and stiff for a while, but you can return to work in a week or two."

"Oh, yes, work. Have you talked with my mom?"

"She and your uncle were here when you came out of surgery. A neighbor came over to stay with your dad. They went back about an hour ago. Your mom said to tell you Wayne has help coming from Wilson Funeral Home in Asheville. They're handling the arrangements for the Willard burials."

"What a way to get business. I'm sure Mom's upset."

"She's just glad you're alive. I sent her and Wayne out the back entrance to avoid the reporters."

"Reporters," I said, emphasizing the plural. "Has the *Gainesboro VISTA* assigned two? That must be half their staff. I can see the headline—'Undertaker Nearly Conducts Own Funeral!'"

"Network reporters, Barry. CNN and at least one other. They've been calling the hospital switchboard trying to reach you."

I stared at Dr. Susan Miller like she had just announced her Martian ancestry.

"I told the switchboard no calls," she said, "and the floor nurses no visitors, except for family. Everyone understands I'll be keeping an eye on you." She gave me another, and this time, lingering kiss.

The telephone rang, breaking the moment.

"So much for doctor's orders," she said. She lifted the receiver and spoke curtly, "Room 237, who's calling please?"

Her face flushed with the slightest hint of red. She cupped her hand over the mouthpiece and offered me the phone. "She says she's your wife. I think I'd better excuse myself."

She left me alone to confront the voice of the woman who still managed to disrupt my life, even by long distance.

"Hello, Rachel."

"My God, Barry. What happened? I heard your name on the news. The news here in Washington. Are you all right?" She sounded so genuinely concerned, I suppressed the sarcastic tone I usually used as defense against her constant criticism of my small-town life.

"Yes. Just got in the way of a little buckshot. I'm sure the press has exaggerated my involvement."

"Don't deny you could have been killed." She sighed. "And people say the cities are dangerous."

After a few seconds of long-distance hum, she went on, "I'm glad you're all right, Barry."

"I know you are, Rachel." There was a knock at the door, and the face of a pirate leered at me. "Sorry, someone's here," I told her. "I've got to hang up. Thanks for the call. I'll give your best to Mom."

"And your dad too," she added. "Even if he doesn't understand."

"Thank you, Rachel," I said, and I meant it. She and I couldn't live together, but there was still a basic bond of caring. In some ways, she had been the victim of my father's Alzheimer's as much as any of us. I had been forced to quit

my job with the Charlotte police department and leave my
graduate studies in Criminal Justice at the University of North
Carolina at Charlotte in order to help Mom and her brother
Wayne care for Dad and run the funeral home. Even Charlotte had been too small for Rachel, and there was no way
she would survive in a mountain town the size of Gainesboro.
The divorce had been sad but polite, and she had carried her
life away to Washington.

The pirate bent over my bed. The upper edge of his black
eye-patch cut diagonally across a bushy brown eyebrow, and
from underneath it, a thin, pale scar sliced over the sharp
cheekbone to the corner of a wide, tooth-filled grin. He fixed
his one eye on my bandaged shoulder.

"Well, now, Barry," said Sheriff Tommy Lee Wadkins in a
gravelly voice. "Mighty thoughtful of you to get shot in a
cemetery. Inconvenient as hell not to die. You feel like telling
me why Dallas Willard wanted to take you out along with
the rest of his family?"

"No," I croaked.

"Hmm," he grunted. "Sounds like you need a drink." He
looked in the empty Styrofoam pitcher, and then brought a
glass of water from the bathroom. "Want to sit up?"

I nodded an "okay" and the sheriff pressed a control button
that set motors whirring. The top half of the bed rose to a
forty-five-degree angle and jerked to a stop.

"Here, sip on this."

I took the glass and let the cool water seep between my
cracked lips. I was acutely aware of the ache in my shoulder
and just as acutely aware that Tommy Lee Wadkins would
not be sympathetic if he thought I had any information he
needed. Pulling a chair beside the bed, the sheriff straddled
it backwards, took a notepad and pencil from the chest pocket
of his desert tan uniform, and stared at me.

"What happened?" I asked, beating him to the question.

He smiled. "Not much. Just the bloodiest mess I've seen
since 'Nam."

Everybody in Gainesboro, or the whole of Laurel County for that matter, knew Lieutenant Tommy Lee Wadkins was a bona fide war hero. He had brought his ambushed platoon through a hellfire, refusing to leave anyone behind. Even though shrapnel to the face had taken an eye and slashed through his cheekbone, the young officer had dragged a dying comrade through the jungle and provided cover while the choppers evacuated his men. Hanging from the skid, he had emptied his magazine as the last chopper lifted him above the smoke and fire to carry him to safety and unwanted glory.

Sheriff Tommy Lee Wadkins never spoke of the war. In all the years I had known him, the word Vietnam never passed his lips until today.

"You're one lucky son of a bitch," he said. "So, we've both been shot, but at least I knew why 'Charlie' wanted to kill me. You got any ideas?"

"Not a clue. You get him?"

Tommy Lee shook his head. "As soon as I got the word, we issued a BOLO."

Since I'd served three years as a patrolman in Charlotte, Tommy Lee freely used cop lingo with me. BOLO. Be on the lookout for.

"Dallas and his truck have disappeared," he said. "A manhunt is underway in four counties and the state has lent a chopper for aerial surveillance. There is no sign he returned to his cabin. He could have gone to earth anywhere within a twenty-mile radius. I figure that's the travel time he had before we got organized."

"He knows these hills," I said.

"As well as anybody. For all we know, he may have an arsenal stored somewhere. I'm hoping this is just some family feud taken to the extreme and he's not a danger to anyone else."

I saw Dallas Willard smiling at me from across the casket. "But I'm not family. I suggest you learn what happened to Dallas Willard during these few days since his grandmother died."

"I've already started. Did you know that last night Dallas filled up an answering machine tape at the mental health clinic?"

"No. Was he trying to reach Dr. Soles?" Dr. Alexander Soles was the psychologist who led a support group for families who were coping with Alzheimer's. Mom and I attended, and Dallas, Norma Jean, and Lee had been a part of it until two weeks ago when Martha Willard's condition took a sharp turn for the worse.

"No, not Dr. Soles," said Tommy Lee. "Dallas Willard was asking for you."

"Me? At the clinic?"

"Yeah, he said he had to reach you and that all he got at the funeral home was an answering service. He said he needed you to tell his grandmother something." Tommy Lee scooted his chair forward as if closer proximity would somehow inspire me to find a sane answer to an absurd question. "Barry, why would Dallas Willard think you could talk to his dead grandmother?"

I shifted on the bed, trying for a more comfortable position that would clear my head. "I don't know. The only times I ever spoke with Dallas were when he came to the Alzheimer's meetings with Lee and Norma Jean."

"You must have said something," Tommy Lee said.

I took another sip of water as I tried to remember the few conversations I had with Dallas. "I first started talking to him a couple of months ago. During one of the sessions, Norma Jean told everyone how Grandma Martha had started calling him Francis."

"Francis?"

"Yeah, for Saint Francis. Martha Willard thought he could talk to the animals. Dallas became very upset. He said that was private. Between him and his grandma. He stormed out of the room. I went after him to try and calm him down. I guess I felt sorry for him."

Tommy Lee looked at his notes. "Alex Soles told me he suspects Dallas is a borderline paranoid/schizophrenic and believes his grandmother's death may have triggered a full-blown psychotic episode."

"Triggered is right." I moved again and felt the pain in my shoulder. "I'd always sensed something odd about him. He had difficulty expressing himself in our sessions. The night he got so upset I found him leaning against the hood of his pickup, crying like a baby."

"Did you say anything to him?"

"I told him not to let what other people said bother him. That it was obvious he had a special relationship with his grandmother just like I did with my father. He said he didn't care about what other people thought. He just didn't like to think of living without Grandma Martha. We talked for a while, and then I asked him to come back inside with me because I didn't want to leave my mother alone. He followed me in as docile as a lamb. At the next meeting, he sat beside me. He would say hello and goodbye only to me and hardly anything else in between."

"He's always been a quiet one," said Tommy Lee, "but then a lot of these mountaineers are. Since he was never in trouble, I never gave him much thought."

"Then he stopped coming altogether. Must have missed three sessions in a row. I asked Norma Jean where he was and she said my guess was as good as hers. She said Dallas spent more and more time alone, wandering off in the woods. Two weeks ago, he came to the last meeting before Martha's general health failed. He sat next to me, and as we were leaving, he caught my arm and asked to speak to me alone. 'Mr. Clayton,' he said, although he was only a couple years younger. 'How do you think a person gets to Heaven?'"

"Where'd that come from?" asked Tommy Lee.

"Out of the blue. We'd never talked about an afterlife in the group sessions."

"What did you tell him?"

"I said I believed each of us has to find God for himself, and that as for me, I tried to be a good person, treated others like I wanted to be treated, and tried not to harm anyone. If I did that, then I felt sure God would take care of me when I died."

Tommy Lee chuckled. "Billy Graham can give thanks you won't be taking over his ministry. What did Dallas say then?"

I paused, remembering the scene in the hallway of the mental health clinic. Dallas had backed away from me and smiled the same strange smile I had seen right before he shot me.

"Well?" prompted Tommy Lee.

"The last words Dallas said to me at the clinic were 'you're a good man, Mr. Clayton.'"

Tommy Lee jotted something in his notepad and asked, "Do you remember the last words he said to you in the cemetery?"

"Remember them? I'll never forget them. He'd just shot Lee and Norma Jean, and he shouted 'they're goin' to Hell, and so am I. You tell Grandma I'll save the land. Tell her I love her.'"

Tommy Lee gave a low whistle as we both reached the bizarre conclusion.

"Dallas meant to send me to Heaven as a personal emissary to talk to his grandmother. He was sending me because he thought he was going to Hell for killing his brother and sister."

"I know it sounds crazy, my friend, but it looks like being a good man nearly got your head blown off." His pencil scribbled across the page. "'I'll save the land.' He'd never said anything about the land before?"

"Never."

"I'll look into it, but the first thing I've got to do is find Dallas," he said, flipping the pad shut.

"And do me a favor," I said as he headed for the door. "Keep me posted."

Tommy Lee and I enjoyed a special kinship. At fifty, he was twenty years my senior, a bridge between the generation of my father and my own. He had led countless funeral processions for Dad in the eighteen years since he was first elected sheriff, and during the past two years, he and I had forged our own friendship. He knew I had given up my own law enforcement aspirations in order to help Mom cope with one of the most painful, heart-wrenching situations a family can face. Alzheimer's is a cruel and malicious disease, stealing the person and leaving the shell as an ever-present reminder of the loss. Tommy Lee understood sacrifice, and for all his teasing, I knew I had his admiration. He didn't have to tell me he was upset that Dallas Willard had nearly gunned me down. I felt confident when Tommy Lee said "I'll look into it," his one eye would see more than any other two in the county.

The nurse came in so quickly that she must have been waiting outside the door. She carried a tray with a hypodermic syringe and a menu for tomorrow's meal selection. I checked off an assortment of bland options and let her assist me in rolling over on my good side.

"Now, Mr. Clayton," she said, "that ought to take the edge off and let you sleep."

She came around to help me lie on my back. "Nurse…" I left the word hanging as I struggled to see her ID badge.

"Carswell, but I go by Millie."

"Millie, would you hand me the phone?"

"I'll be glad to dial for you."

"Just the hospital switchboard."

She punched zero and gave me the receiver.

"Thank you," I said. "I'll be all right."

Millie left as the operator came on the line.

"Is it possible to order flowers out of the hospital?" I asked.

"You have flowers in your room you don't want, sir?" The woman was clearly surprised a patient would make such a request.

"No, I want to order flowers to be delivered elsewhere."

She connected me to the hospital floral shop where the elderly proprietor complimented me on my thoughtfulness. I had him repeat the message for the card. "For Dr. Susan

Miller, at the O'Malley Clinic—Patient Barry Clayton is grateful for her loving care."

I hung up the phone and rewarded myself with sleep.

I awoke to a Saturday morning much like the day before. Low clouds coated what little scenery was visible from my hospital window with a scrim of white. The shoulder still hurt, but the pain had leveled out to an even plateau. There was a creak in the shadowed corner of my room, and Dr. Alex Soles stood up from the visitor's chair. A big bag of Snickers dangled from one hand and a magazine was curled in the other.

"Brought you something to eat and read." He laid his gifts on a table under the window, then pulled the chair closer to the bed but didn't sit down. He grabbed my wrist and gave a gentle squeeze.

"Glad you're in the hospital and not your own funeral home," he said.

"Thanks."

Alex stood for a few seconds, not saying anything. He and I did not know each other well. Outside of the sessions on dealing with Alzheimer's, I had only crossed paths with him a few times at social functions. I pegged him in his late forties. Cordial, professional, and dedicated were adjectives that best described him. Especially dedicated. He had the reputation for being a therapist who calmly and confidently steered others through their own trials.

"Any word on Dallas?" I asked.

He shook his head. "Why in the hell did he do it, Barry?" Alex's eyes locked on mine, and I knew he had submerged his personal feelings for the moment and was professionally struggling for an answer. "You must have some idea. My secretary played the answering machine tape yesterday when I came in at ten. Of all days to have a damn Rotary breakfast meeting."

"What did he say?"

"Dallas just rambled on about how you had to talk to his grandmother. Tell her he'd been cheated. Cheated by his family. I phoned Sheriff Wadkins immediately, but it was too late. The call had just come in from the cemetery."

Again he reached out and squeezed my wrist. "I'm so sorry. I wish I could have gotten to him. He sounded so agitated. Extremely paranoid. So much so that I'd have to say his actions were in keeping with his mental state."

"Can I hear the tape?"

"I turned it over to Sheriff Wadkins. But you're in no condition to worry about it right now."

"I'm in no condition to forget it. The man tried to kill me, Alex."

Alex smiled and sat down in the chair. "We're alike, Barry. You know that?"

"In what way?" I asked.

"We've got to know why people act as they do. That's why you were studying Criminal Justice before your father's illness, isn't it? Curiosity as to why people behave as they do, and how anti-social, illegal behavior can be modified. Psychology and Criminal Justice are linked because when psychology fails, the criminal justice system usually inherits the problem. And you and I both feel guilty that we didn't do enough for Dallas Willard in time."

"Nobody could find him, Alex."

"I mean earlier, before Martha died. Linda Trine mentioned Dallas to me several weeks ago. She handles the social services for a lot of the migrant workers. Seems Dallas kept coming down into the camp accusing them of taking his land. Like they were some foreign invaders. The migrants have been picking for forty years or more. Nothing new about them being here, and Dallas doesn't even have any cleared land in production. Linda thought Dallas needed some help because he'd never acted that way before. That last Alzheimer's session wasn't the appropriate time, and I was swamped with other cases and didn't follow up with him."

"I know other members of the staff must also have people they can't get to, Alex."

"But how many shoot three people?"

"I was afraid these beauties would die if left solely to my care," announced Susan Miller as she came in carrying a basketful of wildflowers, the multitude of blossoms arranged in a kaleidoscope of colors.

"That's comforting," I said. "Do you feel that way about your human patients?"

She ignored the question and cleared a spot on the table by the bag of Snickers and the magazine. "Who thought you needed *Psychology Today?*" she asked.

"Alex Soles was by earlier. Must be from his waiting room. Probably from the last century."

She laughed. "No, for a doctor's office, it's current. Last April." Susan set down the basket of flowers and turned the arrangement to catch what little light came through the window.

"Good. This way I can take care of both of you at the same time," she said. "And thank you. Saturday deliveries aren't cheap."

"I'm billing that portion to my ex-wife."

She came over to the bedside and gave me a kiss. "I know she means well. I stopped by the funeral home and gave your mom an update. She hopes to drop by after lunch. Now let me take a look at my handiwork." She laid her hand on the bandage, testing the security of the wrapping. "O'Malley been in yet this morning?"

"Yes. About an hour ago. He said you had the morning off and I may have to go home today."

"And that's bad?"

"Room service here is better than my cabin. I had to let the butler go. And I don't know where the chauffeur parked my limo. Actually, Mom will insist I come to the funeral home. You know she already spends most of the day waiting on Dad, and I'd just as soon stay here until I can fend for myself."

"Okay, I'll let you rest up one more night, but I'm afraid tomorrow your insurance company throws you out on the street." She winked. "Maybe I'll leave my condo door unlocked."

Chapter 3

Standing in my kitchen, I watched the pure spring water turn the color of dark molasses as it flowed out the coffee filter and splattered against the glass bottom of the Pyrex pot. Steam swirled off the trickling stream and carried the invigorating aroma of freshly ground beans. I took a deep breath and stretched, one hand nearly touching the rough hewn rafters overhead, the other wriggling helplessly against my stomach because that arm was securely taped to my body.

I filled a mug of coffee and took it out on the back deck of the cabin where I could watch the sunrise boil the mist out of the valley below. The morning light seemed touchable, a golden shroud resurrecting life with its soft glow. A pair of gray squirrels chased each other through the branches of a nearby hickory tree, their chatter blending in with the caws of unseen crows who sounded hell-bent on driving some intruder from their territory. I felt just as possessive of my mountain retreat. Growing up, I had taken these ancient hills for granted. It's when you lose something that it becomes more precious. A part of me had always remained here. Even when I rejected my father's funeral business and moved away, I couldn't reject the Appalachian heritage fused to my soul.

I had purchased the cabin and the five-acre tract of land from a psychiatrist in Charleston, S.C. whose own health kept him from making use of what he had planned to be his summer home. Logs had been culled from at least four original cabins scattered across western North Carolina and eastern Tennessee. Their century-plus heritage created a rustic atmosphere that I found rejuvenating after a day of toil at the funeral home. To think that a hundred and fifty years ago a living, breathing man felled the trees and hewed the logs that now gave me shelter put my problems in perspective. These reassembled walls with modern mortar chinked between the timbers enclosed conveniences my woodsmen forefathers could never have imagined.

As I sat in the cool, gentle breeze, I thought about Dallas Willard's final words to me—"I'll save the land." So far, nothing had come to light. A week had passed since the slaughter in the cemetery. Dallas had not been captured, and the reasons for his murderous rampage were no clearer than when I lay bleeding under the shattered gravestone. Speculation grew that he might have committed suicide, except no one had seen his truck and a truck is harder to overlook than a dead body.

It was nearly nine when I went back inside for the last cup in the pot. I had just finished refilling the filter with fresh grounds, no easy task with one hand coming out of your belly button, when I heard footsteps on the gravel outside. My first thought was of Dallas Willard and the sound he made walking across the gravel to his grandmother's casket. With my heart in my throat, I turned to the open front door as the footsteps trod heavily across the porch. Sheriff Tommy Lee Wadkins' familiar face peered through the screen, his one good eye scanning the room. He was in full uniform with the holstered .38 Smith & Wesson revolver prominent on his hip and a smile forced across his lips.

"Good morning, Barry. Sorry to drop in unannounced. How you feeling?"

"I'm okay," I said, hoping I didn't look petrified. "Though I itch like crazy under this tape."

"Anybody else here?" he asked in a whisper.

"Just spit it out. You mean is Susan shacked up with me?"

At least my question drew a laugh. "Hey," said Tommy Lee with a shrug, "you know I turn a blind eye to you and Susan cavorting in sin."

"She had hospital rounds, and for your information, she does not cavort. I just have an occasional night-time medical appointment. I am injured you know."

"If you've found a doctor who still makes house calls, then more power to you. So, you're doing okay?"

"Yes and no. Yes, I'm doing okay because I'm healing like I'm supposed to and Uncle Wayne told me not to worry about the funeral home. No, because I'm going nuts cooped up here while Dallas is out there somewhere. What's happening, Tommy Lee?"

"Well, the department is too small to keep working the hours we've been putting in. Yesterday, I decided to return to normal schedules with Dallas being a top priority yet not consuming all our resources. At least, that was yesterday's plan."

"Something changed?"

"Of course. Always happens when you set your mind in one direction. You get it yanked in another. Dallas Willard's truck showed up."

"Where?"

"Dirt road about five miles from here. Hikers found it and must have remembered it from the description on the news. My deputy Reece Hutchins got their cell call this morning."

"Any sign of Dallas?"

"That's what I'm going to see. Reece is at the scene. Thought maybe you'd like to ride along, if you don't mind missing Oprah."

"Don't worry," I joked. "I set the VCR first thing every morning. So, how come y'all missed the truck?"

"That's the interesting part. We'd already checked and re-checked that road. As recently as yesterday afternoon. Seems like our boy Dallas went for a little drive last night."

I wedged my knee against the dashboard as the patrol car took another sharp jolt from an exposed boulder. The dull ache in my shoulder was beginning to sharpen.

"Dirt road?" I grumbled. "This ain't much more than a two-rut footpath."

"Shouldn't be much farther. Dead ends at the railroad bed. That's how the hikers found the truck. They were walking the tracks."

Another rough and tumble quarter mile passed, then the road curved and we emerged from the forest shadows into the brighter light of a clearing. In the sunshine stood Dallas' rusted red pickup. Beside it was parked another patrol car. Deputy Hutchins stood beside a young man and woman who wore small backpacks and looked rather bewildered. Their fall foliage hike had turned into quite a different outing.

We got out and Reece introduced us to Shane and Liz Colbert. They had started walking the rails from a more accessible crossing a couple miles to the south.

"Glad you folks recognized the truck and phoned us," said Tommy Lee.

"We heard the description on the TV, and we didn't see anybody around," said Shane Colbert. He looked at his wife sheepishly. "We kinda hid in the bushes in case that crazy man came back."

His young wife nodded in agreement and reached out to take his hand.

"You were good to stay. And you were smart to be cautious," said Tommy Lee. He turned to Reece. "What have we got?"

His deputy shook his head. "I walked the tracks a hundred yards in each direction, Sheriff. There ain't no sign of him. It's like he vanished into thin air again."

"I work for a god-damned power company and have no electricity. Otherwise I could offer you some coffee."

The man who introduced himself as Fred Pryor stood outside the door of the construction trailer and made the apology.

"Who backed into it?" asked Tommy Lee.

"I don't know. Happened overnight. I discovered it this morning when I arrived. Just one more thing to deal with." He glared at the nearby utility pole lying askew with its black snaking cable dangling in the dust. Then he looked at my hand dangling from the front of my shirt.

"You were shot up at the Willard funeral, weren't you? Saw it on the news. Damndest thing I've ever heard of."

I studied him more closely. Fred Pryor didn't look like a power company senior executive. He wore a green wind-breaker with an "R P & E" insignia, jeans, and black cowboy boots.

"What the hell got into that boy?" he asked.

"We don't know," said Tommy Lee. "Still looking for him. Something about their land. Borders this project, doesn't it? You had any dealings with the family?"

Pryor's face flushed. I didn't know whether he was insulted or embarrassed that Tommy Lee thought he might associate with the Willards. "Not me. Our real estate division might have talked to them. Their property is part of the watershed, and it could be affected should we decide to raise the lake level."

I looked at Tommy Lee and saw his eye squint. Fred Pryor had gotten his attention.

Tommy Lee and I had driven to the construction project when a search around Dallas' truck proved fruitless. The site was within a few miles of the main rail line and would be a logical destination if Dallas were on the run. I looked beyond our powerless host and down the bulldozed valley to the mammoth wall of gravel and stone rising up at the narrow point between the steep ridges.

Just yesterday, I had read an article in the newspaper about the Broad Creek excavation. The first phase of the hydro-electric project had progressed on schedule and under budget. Soon Broad Creek would be dammed, and as the new lake began to form, Ridgemont Power and Electric would focus on the construction of the facilities, turbines, generators, and network of transmission lines necessary to convert nature's aquatic energy into electricity for the power-hungry consumer.

The article announced Senior Executive Vice President Fred Pryor was personally overseeing the project. It was a challenge that skipped all the political headaches of a nuclear facility, but there were still the environmentalists and EPA inspectors to deal with. "Keeping the project on time and on budget is the company's top priority because Broad Creek is good for the public and good for the shareholders." So said Fred Pryor in the newspaper.

"Ridgemont Power and Electric was buying the land?" Tommy Lee asked.

"Not that I know of. Not my area. I think I saw a memo at the home office that the family didn't want to discuss it while the grandmother was alive. That's understandable. Ol' timers get so attached to their memories."

Except Martha Willard didn't have any memories. Not at the end. But Dallas had so strong an attachment that he murdered his brother and sister. Was that the reason Ridgemont Power and Electric had only gotten as far as inquiries? Had Dallas refused to sell?

"Any leads on where Willard might be?" Pryor asked, changing the subject. "You think he came on our property?"

"We don't know that," said Tommy Lee. "It's just that we found his truck on an old logging road a few miles away. It dead-ends next to the main rail line. You've got a spur running in here. We thought he might have taken it."

The engine whistle broke through the sheriff's comments. We looked up the valley to the track running along the water. The power company's own yard engine rolled along hauling out several carloads of debris to the truck loading zone at the main highway. From there it would bring back more gravel or other construction supplies directly to the dam site.

"That's the old Pisgah Paper Mill's abandoned spur," said Pryor. "Activating it was my idea. It's proven to be a real asset for transporting materials in and out of the valley. We never go all the way out to the main line, and we chain a gate across the track each night. I'll alert the crew to keep their eyes open. Good luck, Sheriff. Nice to have met you, Mr. Clayton. Hope you're on the mend." Tommy Lee and I had been dismissed.

As we walked back to the patrol car, Tommy Lee said, "I don't like him."

"Pryor? Why not?"

"See that blue Mercury parked by the trailer?"

I turned around and stared at the car, one of several parked by the edge of the mobile office. When I noticed the "Cain for Sheriff" bumper stickers plastered all over the rear, I thought I understood why Tommy Lee disliked the man. Cain was challenging him in next month's election. "Maybe it's one of his employees," I said.

"No, it's not," said Tommy Lee. "And it's not Pryor's either. That's my esteemed opponent's car. Bob Cain himself. He does security consulting. Explains why Fred Pryor hustled outside to meet us." Tommy Lee smiled. "The son of a bitch is aiding and abetting the enemy."

"What now?" I asked. "We don't even know which direction Dallas may have headed."

The Sheriff leaned in the open car door and yanked the mike from its cradle. "I'll have the deputies organize search teams. We should walk the tracks."

I looked up at the hills surrounding the excavated valley. Dallas Willard was out there somewhere, mentally unstable, exposed to the elements and dangerous. He had reached out to me for help by phone, and then tried to kill me with his gun. I couldn't stand the idea of being out of the action. A part of me still was and always would be a law officer.

"Count me in," I told Tommy Lee.

He looked at my useless arm.

"Hey. There is nothing wrong with my legs."

He smiled. "No, I guess not. Too bad I can't say the same thing about your head."

Chapter 4

The next day was a cool and breezy Saturday. Reverend Lester Pace and I were hiking along a five-mile rail spur that ran to an abandoned quarry. Friday afternoon's search had netted no sign of Dallas in the immediate area. The truck yielded no clues, and there were no missing person or stolen vehicle reports to indicate Dallas had hijacked someone on departing the scene. Tommy Lee had checked with the Norfolk-Southern and the CSX rail lines. Neither reported trouble with any of their freights running along that stretch. It was as if, as Deputy Hutchins had said, Dallas had vanished into thin air. The search was being conducted regardless, and Tommy Lee had coordinated groups of officers from other counties with his own team, pairing the searchers so no one worked alone or without someone familiar with the area. A few civilian volunteers were included who knew the coves and hollows, but each was instructed to adhere to any orders or commands issued by the accompanying law officer. Tommy Lee's goal was to comb the rail lines within a thirty-mile radius of Dallas' truck.

Pace and I were the exceptions. Tommy Lee had reluctantly given into my request to be a part of the search because he respected the training I had received on the Charlotte force. He teamed me with Reverend Pace because Pace knew the area as well as anyone, and he too wouldn't take no for an answer. We were given a dead-end stretch of track and told to stay on it. Tommy Lee insisted we be armed for our own protection. I carried my five-shot .38 Smith & Wesson Special high on my hip. Tommy Lee also insisted that if we saw any sign that Dallas might be or had been in the vicinity, we were to summon up the proper authorities to take further action.

Of all the preachers I dealt with in the funeral business, Pace was my favorite. He had been a Methodist circuit-rider for over forty years. Time might have lessened his step but not his stamina. He carried a twisted rhododendron trunk as a walking stick, which he brandished like a drum major marshaling the band. Although the temperature couldn't have been above forty-five, I worked up a sweat matching stride with him. As we walked along the rusted steel rails, the preacher searched the right side of the gravel bed and I took the left.

"Haven't seen your Dad in about a month, Barry. How's he doing?" Pace asked the question after we'd covered a couple miles and thoroughly talked out the shooting at Crab Apple Valley Baptist Church and the possible reasons for Dallas Willard's actions. It was not lost on Pace that the missing man was mentally disturbed and needed compassion along with capture. Pace's compassion was genuine; so was the .32 Colt tucked in his belt.

"Dad is more frightened," I said. "Stays upstairs most of the time. A few steps out in the hall and he forgets where he is going. Forgets where he is. And there are times he looks at me and can't quite place my face."

The old preacher shook his head. "Alzheimer's is a hell of a thing. Hardest on the ones closest. God give you strength."

I didn't say anything. I didn't want God's strength. I wanted Him to take this curse off my father, the gentlest man who ever lived. Pace read my thoughts.

"Your father is quite courageous. You know that?"

"Yes," I replied tersely.

"A few years ago, he told me he had only one fear. That fear wasn't for himself. He knows his death will come through a painless oblivion. His fear is for you."

"Me?" I stammered before I could stop myself.

"He's afraid you will become bitter. Bitter that your love for him and your mother disrupted your own life. Brought you back to the small town and the job you had no interest in having. He has accepted you wanted more than Gainesboro could give and that he would not pass the funeral business on to you like your grandfather had handed it to him. But then, it happened." Pace took a deep breath and seemed to stare back five years to that dreadful day when the whole town realized something was wrong with my father.

Mother had called in tears. Dad had been driving the limousine behind the hearse en route to Good Shepherd Cemetery when, to the shock of the grieving family, he pulled out of the procession and passed both the hearse and Tommy Lee's escorting deputy as he leaded. Dad had forgotten where he was and what he was doing. A host of doctors and tests yielded a diagnosis that was more of a slow death sentence: Alzheimer's at age fifty-five, an age struck by fewer than three percent of the cases and a statistic of brutal consequences. For three years, he and Mom struggled to keep the business going while seeking someone to take it over. Uncle Wayne, Mom's brother and a man older than my father, had neither the ambition nor the finances to buy it. No other individual came forward with an offer, and none of the big chains were interested. The burden fell to me.

Pace spoke again. "You have my respect, Barry, for what you did. But, if it turns you against yourself and against your God, then you should make every effort to sell and go back to the life that made you happy."

"What life," I said. "My wife wouldn't follow me here. So much for 'for better or for worse.' What do I have to look forward to? Going back to working nights on the Charlotte police force? Re-enrolling at the university in a foolish quest for a Masters? Chasing some half-baked notion of working for the FBI? No one should feel sorry for me or worry about me, Preacher. I'm not the one whose personality is being erased each day. I'm not the one whose body will be a living shell of the man who won't remember being husband or father." I felt the words choke me up, and I stopped walking and looked away.

"And you've no one to lash out at but God," he said. "I understand and God understands. He's there for you and He can lift the anger off of you. Take comfort."

"Here's my comfort," I said, sweeping my good arm in an arc wide enough to encircle the ridges surrounding us. The fall colors—orange, red, and yellow—blazed across their backs and the ice-blue sky arched over them like an infinitely deep canopy. "I take comfort in this. No offense, but they speak louder than any sermon I've ever heard."

Pace looked at the panorama surrounding us. "They latch onto you, don't they? These mountains."

"Yes," I agreed. "Yes, they do. Despite my efforts to escape them."

"But it's the people hidden in the coves and hollows who keep me here. The people your father has served all his life." He started walking again, slower, and he spoke in a cadence matching his stride.

"Whenever I get discouraged or think that God has abandoned me, the people hold me. First time it happened, I'd been here only six months. One Sunday morning in a little shack of a church near Hickory Nut Falls—chicken coop churches folks used to call them—I finished my last service for the day. Back then, I'd preach over in Yellow Mountain community at eight in the morning, hop in my forty-eight Plymouth coupe and high-tail it like a bat off the devil's doorstep to Eagle Creek for nine-thirty worship, and then be in Hickory Nut Falls at eleven. There were only ten to fifteen families in each congregation."

"Chicken coops?"

Pace laughed. "When I say 'chicken coop,' I'm not straying from the God's truth. The church was a combination of old plank boards, tar paper, and tin roofing that a couple of the families had pulled together from their own houses.

"No cross, no white steeple, no sign out front with my name and this week's sermon topic. Just a shelter from Life's storm where these folks could escape their poverty and hardship for an hour and praise God for the simple joys money can't buy. Inside, the pews were only wooden benches, the pulpit was a post with a board nailed to it, and the music was whoever happened to bring a dulcimer or guitar. I wanted to build a real church and fill the pews, but it wasn't happening. I was down on myself and down on the calling. I'd petitioned the bishop for a new assignment."

"Bet he didn't want to hear it," I said.

"I wasn't the first young pup old Bishop Wallace had to train. He said he'd pray about it, which meant I couldn't complain while a divine response was in the making.

"Several weeks later, after Sunday service, I boxed up my Bible and the hymnbooks I carried from church to church, though most of the congregation couldn't read. A few folks came up to talk with me, mostly some of the ladies and their young-uns as the men tended to hold back or even sit outside during the preaching and singing. Like I said, I'd only been here a little while, so people were a little gun-shy.

"When I thought everyone had left, I lifted up the box with the Bible and hymnals and walked down the narrow aisle to the front door. Just before I reached it, a man stepped in the doorway blocking my path. He was about six-foot tall, lean as a twig, wearing a beat-up pair of overalls and gray, sweat-stained work shirt. Pushed back atop his head was an old, floppy-brimmed, brown felt hat. A squirrel rifle lay across his folded arms. I especially noticed the squirrel rifle."

"Guess he didn't like the sermon," I interrupted.

Reverend Pace smiled. "That's what I thought, Barry. I took some comfort that the hammer wasn't cocked. Yet.

"'Preacher, you in a hurry?' he asked.

"I had never seen him before. Didn't know if he was one of the men who sat outside, but I did know that in my six-months experience, no one brought a gun to church.

"'No, not particularly,' I said. 'Can I help you?'"

Pace stopped walking and leaned on his stick. His eyes held mine and his smile disappeared. "What I at first thought was meanness in his face melted with my offer. I realized the old man was tensed up over something. Evidently, I could help. I felt the pastoral call to feed the flock.

"'I'd be obliged if you'd come back to the house with me. I got a burial needs tendin' to.' He looked at the box in my arms. 'Bring the Good Book.'

Pace laughed and started walking again. "Well, now there's nothing more confounded than a speechless preacher. I must a looked like every bit of sense had been snatched from my head. At last I stammered, 'But has the body been prepared? Paperwork filled out and everything?'

"'All ready,' he said. He looked down at his feet, ashamed to meet me eye to eye. 'I ain't learnt enough to say the words. Ain't no church goer.'

"Having made his confession, he made his demand. 'So, you goin' to help?'

"Now I'd done a few burials, and even interred one on family property with your dad, but never an impromptu funeral. I didn't know what to say, but I sure didn't say no. Just nodded my head and followed that mountaineer outside."

A flash caught my eye along the edge of the rail bed. I jumped back toward Pace. "Wait," I said. "I see something." In my mind, it was a glint off Dallas Willard's shotgun.

We stood silently for several seconds. The only sounds came from a chorus of blue jays. Then somewhere down the track a squirrel chattered.

Pace and I ventured back to the edge of the crossties. Instinctively, he stepped away from me so that one shotgun blast could not take both of us. I carefully stepped down the gravel rail bed. While Pace covered me, I grabbed a handful of green mountain laurel leaves and lifted the branch.

"Beer cans," I said with relief. "Can you believe it? We're two miles from nowhere and here are the relics of a party."

"I'm surprised the astronauts didn't find beer cans when they landed on the moon," said Pace. "You got good eyes, Barry."

He extended his walking stick so that I could grab the tip and steady my climb up to the track.

"Yeah, good eyes but bad nerves," I said. "Sorry. I left you facing a real gun in church."

"Like I said, nothing like this had never happened before. A command performance at a funeral. So, this old man and I stepped out of the church and all I saw was my Plymouth and the cornfield down to the creek. I knew he had walked out of the hills.

"'Can we drive to your place?' I asked.

"'Partly,' he answered.

"We got in the Plymouth and drove off. Me and the old mountain man, the Bible and hymnals bouncing between us. He never spoke. Just pointed the turn at each crossroads. The pavement became gravel, the gravel became dirt, until finally two ruts were all that marked what had been an old wagon trail. I stopped the car, afraid to push my luck any farther.

"'Don't forgit the Good Book,' he reminded me.

"We walked up the ridge on an overgrown footpath till we came to a little clearing of a couple acres of pasture. In the middle was his cabin. Shack, I should say. Front porch roof propped up with small tree trunks, bark still on them. Side planking had been covered in black tar paper for weathering. It was torn through in places and I saw cracks in the slats through to the inside. In front, a few chickens and guinea hens scratched for grubs. No other sign of life.

"We walked around the side by a pile of cordwood. A couple wedges and an axe lay up under some of the logs. In the back, a well-traveled path led from the rear of the cabin to the outhouse, its door half off makeshift hinges. Over at the edge of the clearing, about thirty yards away, was a freshly dug hole. Maybe three foot by four foot. The dirt was heaped up beside it with a shovel lying atop the pile. At the far edge of the hole, I saw an old tattered tarp stretched out over something and weighed down with stones.

"A chill rippled down my spine, and I shuddered in horror at the size of the tarp.

"'My God,' I thought. 'It's a child. This man has lost a child.'

"Calling up every ounce of courage, I followed him over to the grave site. I braced as he bent down and pulled back the tarp. There before me lay the mangiest ol' coon dog I've ever seen. His eyes glassed over and body stiff as a board. His legs were so straight and rigid, I swear to God, if you'd set him up, he could have been a footstool.

"All the fear, the dread that had built up inside me since the stranger blocked my doorway busted loose and I did one of the meanest things I've ever done in my life. I laughed. Laughed till I thought my insides would pop loose.

"I heard the squirrel gun cock. The sound snapped me out of my hysteria.

"The man stood up from bending over the dead animal. He glared at me with a look of hurt and hate. The gun barrel pointed straight at my belly.

"'That's Roddey,' he said. 'The finest friend I ever had.' He held the rifle in one hand and removed his hat with the other. Tears ran along the creases in his weathered cheeks. 'Am I goin' to have to dig this hole bigger?'

"My heart stopped. I must have gone white as a sheet. I don't know what kept me from passing out and falling into the hole. I felt my knees start to give on me and my hands were shaking so much I could hardly get the Bible open." Pace smiled at the memory.

Looking at the white-haired preacher with a staff in his hand and pistol in his belt, I found it hard to imagine him as once being terrified.

"But I found passages of Scripture I didn't know I could find. We went through the birds of the air, beasts of the field, lions laying down with lambs, anything that had an animal, I read.

"Then I prayed for Ol' Roddey—the finest dog that ever lived. It was somewhere in the prayer—two prayers actually, the vocal one for Roddey, the silent one for me—that I heard him uncock the gun. I said a few more 'Thank you, Lords' from the bottom of my heart and we committed Roddey's carcass back to the mountain."

Reverend Pace shook his head, then started walking again, carefully placing his rhododendron stick on the crossties. "Yeah, we covered Roddey up and the old man asked me into the cabin. He and I shared some corn—liquor that is," he added with a chuckle. "As a Methodist, I considered it medicine to calm my nerves. Only then did he tell me his name. Jake McGraw.

"You see, Barry, I'd performed a spiritual function for Jake no one in my seminary class could have imagined. I was an outsider, but Jake McGraw needed me. Praying over Roddey was doing the Lord's work. I understand that now. After that, Ol' Jake came down every Sunday and sat on the back corner of the back bench. He was still a strange old hermit, but in his own way, he gave me a stamp of approval. Believe me, it didn't go unnoticed by the other mountain folk. In a year, Hickory Nut Falls was my largest congregation. Today, there is a church there instead of a chicken coop. And a parking lot too.

"Ten years later, your dad and I buried Jake beside Ol' Roddey. And I swear at the final 'Amen,' a coon dog howled from the mountain top."

"Yeah, right," I laughed. "You're doing a number on me."

"It's true," said Pace. "You can ask Charlie. He was a friend of Jake's."

The preacher pointed to a break in the bordering pines. I saw a field sloping away from us. Halfway down the hillside, a massive workhorse plodded along. Behind him, with both hands guiding the wooden plow, a skinny man in blue bib-overalls stepped over the clods of freshly turned earth. The old guy was eighty if a day.

"That's Charlie Hartley," said Pace.

"Don't believe I know him."

"Well, you're about to." He swung the walking stick in the air and caught the farmer's attention. The man pulled back on the reins and hollered "whoa-up." The gentle beast lumbered to a halt and snorted his displeasure. He shook his head, twisting his neck around the sweat-stained collar to roll an eye toward the barn at the far end of the field.

"Charlie's never had a tractor touch his soil. Got no use for them. His horses are his children." The preacher left the railroad tracks and started across the field. "Come on," he said. "Rude not to talk a spell."

"Hello, Reverend," said Charlie. He wiped the sweat from his hands with a red bandanna and grasped Pace's right one with both of his own. "Good to see you." He looked me over. "They finally get you some help?" he asked Pace.

The Reverend laughed. "Yeah, but he ain't it. This is Barry Clayton. He's Jack Clayton's boy. Barry got shot up at the Willard funeral last week."

"Heard something about that," he said with a nod. "You work with your pa?"

"They don't call me Buryin' Barry for nothing."

The old man didn't crack a smile at the joke I'd been saddled with since junior high. He turned to his horse like Pace had turned to me.

"This is Ned. He's paying for his pleasure. Told him last February he shouldn't have jumped Nell. With her foaling just a couple months off, it's just him and me to ready the winter field." He turned and lectured the animal. "Remember that next spring 'fore you go mountin' your plowmate."

The horse flipped his tail as if to say "lay off." Charlie
chuckled at the big stallion's rebuttal. "Course you are giving
me a grandchild of sorts. Guess I should be grateful." He
reached into his shirt pocket for a sugar cube, and, as the
horse took the treat, Charlie scratched the coarse hair between
his dapple ears.

"What are you fellows doing walking in on the Hope
Quarry spur?"

"Guess you didn't know Dallas Willard's still missing,"
said Pace.

"Nope. Ain't been to town since Monday."

"He hasn't been seen since the shooting. Then his truck
shows up yesterday by the railroad about two miles south of
where the quarry spur splits off. Search parties spent today
combing half the county."

"Anything I can do?"

"We could use your phone to check in. After we walk
down to the quarry."

"How much farther is it?" I asked.

"Couple hundred yards," said the preacher.

"I'll do it," I said. "You call the Sheriff's office."

"I'll take Ned to the stall," said Charlie. "Come get me
when you're ready."

On my return, I walked into the shadows of the old barn.
The sound of my footsteps died in the carpet of brown hay
strewn over the dry, packed earth. The rich pungent odor of
manure, sweat, and feed rose up like a barricade. I stopped
for a moment while my eyes adjusted to the dim light.

Against the golden backdrop of the barn's open rear door,
I saw the motionless silhouettes of Reverend Pace and Charlie.
They sat on barrels and watched the mare drink from her
water trough. The barn odor mellowed into an aroma of age.
With reluctance, I intruded upon their silent pleasure.

"I didn't find anything," I said. "You talk to Tommy Lee?"

"Yeah, patched through the two-way radio. Nothing."

"Great day in the morning," muttered Charlie. "What's the sheriff planning?"

"To keep looking at least through the weekend," said Pace. "It's about all he can do. National Park Rangers have agreed to scout park land at Montgomery Rock and Black Bear Bluff. Sheriff's got a couple of the mountain families to do the same on their own land. He hopes somebody will find some sign. Maybe a campfire. Dallas could be lost if he wandered too far into the gorges."

Charlie Hartley kicked the dirt with his work boot. "Tarnation. He's a local boy who knows these hills as well as anybody. He's been up and down them since he could crawl. He ain't lost. If he ain't dead, he's bad hurt. Dogs. Ought to bring in dogs."

"Tried that," I said. "Tommy Lee got the SBI to bring them to the truck. No use. Nothing for the dogs to follow. Scent ended at the tracks. Said Dallas may as well have caught a train."

"Maybe he hopped a freight," said Charlie.

"Railroad told Tommy Lee that would be impossible," I said. "It's not a crossing, and they're usually going thirty-five to forty miles an hour. SBI ran aerial surveillance over the tracks, but it's not as effective as walking the ground, which is what I guess we'd better get back to doing."

Pace stood and clasped a hand on Charlie's shoulder. "Take care of Nell, you hear."

"You come up and see her colt."

"Sure. I kiss all the new babies."

Pace picked up his walking stick and followed me out of the barn, leaving Charlie to lean against the stall and admire his mare.

I knew something was wrong as soon as Pace and I got to the funeral home. From the high corner eaves, the spotlights blazed even though the sky still held the last purple rays of twilight. They were the sign of official business, the illumination for visitors and mourners going to and from the circle of grief.

"Uncle Wayne told me nothing was scheduled for this Saturday night," I said. "That's why we invited you to stay over."

Pace glanced at me as he slowed my Jeep to a crawl.

"Maybe you've got company," he said.

We saw the old blue pickup with dented aluminum camper-top parked at the edge of the pavement. Next to it was a rusted Chevy Nova. "No, not the social kind," I answered. "And I don't see Uncle Wayne's car. I'd better not leave until we know what's going on."

We walked through the side yard to the back porch off the kitchen. My mother bustled out of the door, waving her arms in frantic ellipses, her plump body bobbing up and down as she exhorted us into the house.

"Oh, Barry," she whispered. "It's awful. Just awful. And Wayne's not back from looking for Dallas Willard."

Pace gently held her by the shoulders to calm her. "It's all right, Connie. Tell us what happened."

Her voice quivered and she blinked back tears. "They brought him in the back of a truck. Wouldn't even call for the ambulance."

"Who, Connie?"

"The mother and father. And a neighbor too. He was just a boy. An eight-year-old boy."

"You'd better go on in, Barry," said Pace. "We'll be there in a moment."

As I entered the foyer, I heard whispered voices coming from the viewing room on the left, the one more comfortably called the Slumber Room. I was surprised that Mom had not left the family across the hall in the living room where the homey, informal atmosphere could put the relatives more at ease as they discussed funeral arrangements. The Slumber

Room was reserved for visitation when the family greeted friends and neighbors coming to extend sympathy.

A young woman sat hunched in a straight-backed chair, her face buried in her hands. She wore a threadbare cotton dress and should have added at least a sweater or a jacket for the autumn chill. At her side stood a slender man whose face still bore the marks of adolescent acne. His jeans hung on his hipless body like rags on an understuffed scarecrow. His brown eyes were puffed with red circles, and though the tears no longer flowed, he had to clear his throat before he could speak.

"You Mr. Clayton?" he asked, skeptical of my youthful appearance. "We were told to ask for Jack Clayton." What little weight he had he shifted from foot to foot in nervous agitation. The woman looked up and stared through me, revealing a thin face with translucent skin. Her features could be taken as childlike from a distance, but the sunken eyes and flat cheekbones told of age beyond her years.

"No, I'm his son, Barry."

"Then would you find him," ordered a voice from the back of the room.

Out of the shadows where the dark green drapes hung behind the casket viewing area stepped a man. Light first caught his brown hair, scraggly and dirty, dropping over his shoulders like twisted strands of Spanish moss. The face had a gray pallor, created by unshaven stubble. His pale blue eyes looked out of place beneath heavy dark-brown eyebrows that merged together over his sharp, hooked nose. He raised an oversized black Bible in one hand, letting the scuffed leather cover fall open as if he expected the words themselves to leap from the page.

"The Lord has need of him," he proclaimed. He swept the Bible in a wide arc toward the couple. "There is nothing more we can do but praise His Holy Name."

The woman shook with silent sobs.

"My father is ill," I said. "I'll take care of things."

Beyond the path of the Bible, I saw the child lying on the low oak pedestal where a casket would rest. The small body was stretched out, hands across the chest, face slightly canted toward the wall as if a mischievous boy mocked the solemnity of the grown-ups. I pushed past the Bible-toting neighbor and stood over the child. Dull quarters rested on his eyes, opaque monocles closing out a world filled with new wonder. With my good arm, I lifted them from his face one at a time. There was no need for such nonsense. The child's eyes were shut forever.

"Those are mine," said the belligerent man.

The coins slipped from my fingers and scattered across the hardwood floor. The Bible slammed shut as the man chased after his money. Other footsteps sounded from the hall, and I heard Reverend Pace's gentle voice introducing himself. The father responded "Luke and Harriet Coleman" and the other man said "Leroy Jackson." Then the murmur of conversation blended into a background hum as I focused all my attention on the boy. The sneakers a size too big, yet worn enough to have belonged to someone before him. Jeans rolled up in double cuffs, patches at the knees. A brown belt with scratched silver buckle shaped like a cowboy's six-shooter. A sweatshirt decorated with a montage of Saturday morning super-heroes, animals or aliens, I didn't know which, but a new cast of characters that had become the coveted property of eight-year-olds.

The boy's face carried a layer of summer tan beneath the dirt. A shock of coarse brown hair spread over his forehead while an untamed cowlick sent strands in a rooster tail against the polished wood of the pedestal. The twist of the mouth and the colorless lips drawn back over his teeth were chilling signs of the child's final moments of pain and fear. I reached out and turned his face toward me. Two puncture wounds marred the taut skin just below the right ear. The purple swollen neck rose up like a demon's brand, claiming the child in sadistic triumph.

"What happened?" I spoke to the room, cutting through the voices and sobs, demanding an answer. "What happened to this child?"

My eyes darted to each of them. Reverend Pace stepped closer to see for himself. The neighbor looked from me to the boy's mother and father. He gave a slight nod.

"Snakebite," replied the father. He steadied himself by resting his hand on his wife's shoulder. She stared at the floor. "Rattlesnake. Jimmy was playing on some rocks near the house. Musta crawled up under a ledge. We heard him screaming." The man's voice faltered. He looked at Leroy Jackson.

"I was just driving up to their house when it happened," said Jackson. "The boy was gone in a matter of minutes. I was the one killed the snake. It's out in the truck."

"Did you call a doctor?" I asked. "There should have been more time."

"No phone. And I couldn't put no tourniquet round the kid's neck, now could I."

"Call Ezra Clark," I told my mother. "It's required procedure," I explained to the others. "He'll need to sign a coroner's statement."

"I don't want him cuttin' on my Jimmy," said Luke Coleman. His wife started sobbing again.

Mother started for the telephone, then hesitated. "Barry, we should get Travis McCauley."

"Who's that?" asked Leroy Jackson. "We don't need a lot of people in here gawkin'."

"Mr. McCauley runs a furniture store," I said. "He also makes a few caskets. We don't have one appropriate for this child."

The father cleared his throat again. "I'm afraid we're kinda short on cash money."

"That can wait, Mr. Coleman. I'll make the calls to the coroner and Mr. McCauley. This boy deserves a decent burial."

"My wife and I'll be carrying him back to Kentucky," said Luke Coleman. "It's where my wife's people are buried."

"Certainly," I said. "But first there are necessary things we have to do regardless of where he's going to be interred. I suggest you and your wife follow my mother back to the kitchen for a cup of tea. We can talk about those arrangements there."

Then my mother said something that made me want to hug her. "And Mr. Jackson, I suggest you either be of comfort to these good people or you be quiet."

"Sorry, I've done it again." I made the apology as soon as Susan opened her front door. "I really couldn't say much on the telephone. I was standing in Mom's kitchen."

She nodded. "I hope you didn't look as pitiful as you do now. Well, our dinner reservations are beyond salvaging, and I expect you're in no mood for a night on the town. You may as well stay awhile."

I went to my customary spot, an overstuffed armchair across from the sofa.

Fifteen minutes later, I still sat in the armchair, but my clothes sloshed in the washing machine, and a beer sloshed down my throat. Susan convinced me of the wisdom in spending the night in Gainesboro and then going straight to the sheriff's office at dawn to rejoin the search for Dallas. I pulled the terry-cloth bathrobe tighter around my waist so that I could rest the ice-cold beer bottle on my lap without singing soprano.

"I just couldn't leave those people," I began.

Susan stretched out on the sofa opposite me. She had changed into a silk dressing gown and wrapped her delicate surgeon's hands around a long-stemmed glass of white wine. Her dark brown eyes stared at me over the rim of the glass. I would willingly lie on any operating table if that angelic face were looking down at me.

"Of course, you couldn't," she said.

"Uncle Wayne came in a few minutes after I called you. He'd been walking track in the northern part of the county. He's no spring chicken, and he and his partner tried to cover too much ground. He was exhausted, but he still came back to the mess at the funeral home as soon as he got word."

"The Colemans. Does anybody know them?"

"No. They've been down from Kentucky about a year. Luke Coleman is on the crew clearing the Broad Creek dam site. Ten or so families migrated here to work on the project. Evidently, the power company has let them build a shanty commune on some of their land. They keep to themselves. And Jimmy, the little boy"—I paused as I saw the child's face in my mind—"the family's adamant about no autopsy."

"Well," said Susan, "that's understandable. I've witnessed enough to know the procedure is pretty dehumanizing. If it were a child of mine, I don't know how I'd react. No question about the snakebite? Ol' Ezra Clark is not the sharpest coroner in the world."

"We saw the rattler. It was huge, over six feet, and the venom must have gone directly into the jugular. This Leroy Jackson, their neighbor, smashed its head with a stone. Snake blood was all over the front seat of his truck from where he tossed it in. Still writhing according to him. He quoted the old wives' tale about snakes not truly dying until sundown. If there were any question about the cause of the boy's death, an autopsy would be mandatory. Ezra said it's pointless to put the mother and father through that ordeal."

"What happens now?" asked Susan.

"Wayne put a call into a funeral home in Harlan, Kentucky. He's making arrangements for transportation of the body and he's coming in tomorrow for the embalming. We agreed I'd do more good looking for Dallas. Tomorrow night at seven-thirty there will be a short visitation. You'll be gone by then."

"Me?" Susan's eyebrows arched into question marks.

"Mom's invited you for dinner. At six. It would really cheer her up."

"And you knew I just couldn't say no," Susan said, stealing the words from my lips.

"Wayne will be there, getting ready for the Colemans. And Reverend Pace. He's staying in town for some meeting with his Bishop. I'll be back from the search by then. With luck, tomorrow we'll find Dallas and this will become just an unwanted souvenir." I patted my wounded shoulder. The beer did wonders for the itch.

Chapter 5

Reverend Pace blessed more than the food. Starting with the Creator, in five terse sentences he moved from the cosmos through the plant and animal kingdoms, across the fields of the farmers, to the God-given culinary talents of my mother.

"Amens" echoed around the table. I opened my eyes to see Pace looking at Fats McCauley. Pace must have been watching him while the rest of us sat with heads bowed and eyes closed. "Soul-tending," my grandmother would have called it: the ability to see a troubled spirit.

The serving dishes heaped with Sunday fixings began their clockwise loop around the dining room table. Mom could have fed three times as many as the six of us. Dad had eaten earlier up in his room. More than a few people around him made him nervous.

By the time I had gotten home from the search party, showered, put on a coat and tie, and picked up Susan, we had been nearly fifteen minutes late. Again, the hunt for Dallas had yielded nothing. Since Reverend Pace had had to preach at his churches and meet with his Methodist Bishop, Tommy Lee had paired me with Deputy Hutchins. We scoured more than ten miles of the main line track between Gainesboro and Asheville.

The trek had been exhausting. Not that the physical effort was that great. It was the tension. Any bend in the track, any depression in the roadbed could have concealed the man who tried to kill me. I had felt both frustration and relief when, mid-afternoon, the bottom of the gray heavens opened, and a cold, brittle rain drenched us. Neither Reece nor I could have gone any farther. We had walked back a half mile to my Jeep, and I had driven the deputy to his patrol car parked at Allied Concrete's rail yard, the spot where we had begun our search. The two-vehicle shuttle had saved the time and effort of hiking all the way back to the start.

The rain still beat against the dining room window, but I was no longer wet and cold. I was starving. Fortunately, I stared at a table laden with Thanksgiving proportions.

Mother had included Fats McCauley at the Sunday evening feast. He and my Uncle Wayne had brought the Coleman boy's casket over by hearse, and it had been easy to convince Fats to stay for dinner. All of us called him Travis to his face, but at three-hundred-plus pounds, "Fats" was the nickname most commonly heard around town.

When the dinner plates had been smothered in fried chicken, coleslaw, crisp cornbread muffins, and mounds of mashed potatoes coated with brown gravy, the flow of conversation trickled to limited exchanges of observations on the weather and compliments on the food. My mother, satisfied that each had been well-served, joined in the discussion.

"Was your meeting this afternoon important?" she asked Pace.

The preacher looked up from a drumstick and laughed. His face cracked into hundreds of weathered crevices, and he pushed back the strands of gray hair that dangled from his high forehead. "Are you saying some Methodist meetings are unimportant, Connie?"

Mom blushed. She knew he was teasing, but his question embarrassed her. "Oh, no," she rallied. "I'm sure it was very important if the bishop himself came."

"Yeah, that old coot," said Pace. "If Gabriel sounded his trumpet tonight for Judgment Day, Bishop Richards would organize a committee for how the Methodists should respond. We'd be the last in line at the Pearly Gates."

"No," said Fats. "If it were Bingo night, the Catholics would be behind the Methodists. Especially if they held double cards."

"At least a Bingo game ends," said Pace. "Well, I'm not being very Christian now, am I? The bishop is all right. Somebody has to make the tough decisions and weigh their theological implications. He leaves me free to wander the mountains serving my three little churches." The Reverend took a second bite from the drumstick.

"And the meeting?" asked Susan.

Pace smiled as he swallowed. "Should have known I couldn't duck the question. The bishop is assigning a young seminary graduate to assist me. Just for a couple months. You know, ride the circuit, get out of the classroom and into the flock."

"Who is he?" Susan asked.

Reverend Pace winked at me. "Quite a sexist assumption. It's 'who is she?'"

"A woman? A woman preacher?" Fats McCauley's eyes widened at the astonishing prospect.

"I haven't actually seen her," replied Pace, "but the name Sarah Hollifield implies we won't be sharing the same tailor." The Preacher rubbed the lapel of his worn tweed sport coat. "She's driving over from Asheville with the bishop tomorrow. I'm not sure he is so keen on the idea of a woman ministering to the mountain folk, but she applied and it would reflect poorly on modern Methodism if she were denied the assignment."

"What do you think?" asked Susan.

"If the mountaineers accepted me, a wet-behind-the-ears Duke graduate, forty years ago, anything is possible. Sarah Hollifield will get my full support. God's work is done by a multitude of hands, male and female."

"God moves in mysterious ways, doesn't She," said Susan.

"Humph," grunted Pace. "I'll leave that question for the Bishop and a committee."

The business telephone rang as Mother served coffee and apple cobbler. Wayne excused himself, slid back from the table, and glided into the adjoining room. His lanky, thin frame was what the locals described as "a tall drink of water" or "high pockets."

Uncle Wayne and my parents were a disappearing breed. They personally cared for the funeral needs of their community in much the same way Reverend Pace cared for the spiritual needs of his flock. They were not employees of a large chain of funeral homes. Mom and Dad literally lived where they worked. Their ante-bellum, white-columned house, set off the street on a gently sloping lawn, was a beautiful home in the tradition of family residences and town funeral businesses. I had rejected both the home and the business when I moved to Charlotte. Clayton and Clayton Funeral Directors was a dying entity in more ways than one.

In a few minutes, Wayne returned, his normally pale complexion flushed. "That was Freddy Mott. He was coming in to help us tonight, but he thinks his distributor cap has got moisture in it. Must be the rain. He can't get his car started." Wayne glanced at his wristwatch. "The Colemans will be here in less than thirty minutes."

"I'm planning to stay," I said.

"We can all help," offered Pace. He stood up and tossed his white linen napkin on the table. "Make us earn our supper."

Mom barred everyone from the kitchen. Even Fats McCauley offered to help with the dishes, but she would hear nothing of it. "The rest of you get things ready for the Colemans," she ordered. "I'll work faster alone."

Susan arranged silk flowers in the Slumber Room and set out a "Those Who Called" book. Wayne and I wheeled in the casket on a rolling cart and Reverend Pace helped at my end to transfer it to the pedestal. We removed the lid and stopped for a moment to look at the boy. Pace said a spontaneous prayer.

The child appeared to be sleeping. Last night my mother had washed and mended his clothes. Gone was the swelling and discoloration from the snakebite. He looked as if a call from his Mom or Dad, or the bark of his dog, would set him in motion, sneakers skimming across the ground in pursuit of a new day.

Fats had had the child's coffin in his inventory. It had been meticulously crafted as a final cradle, a work of art to ease a family's pain that could never go away. The size was right. I hated the thought of a little boy lost in the wide span of satin and ruffles that adults required.

Fats ran a soft cloth over the brass corner trim, wiping clean the dull haze of polish residue. The stillness of the moment was broken by his muffled sob. He turned away, his eyes brimming with tears.

"Y'all leave now," a voice called from the doorway. Leroy Jackson stood with his Bible under his arm and swept his gaze across the room. No one moved. "I said you should leave. You ain't needed. I'm here on behalf of the Lord."

Reverend Pace stepped from behind the casket. He laid his hand on my arm as he passed, signaling me to keep my temper in check. I felt Pace quiver and feared if anyone lost his temper, it would be he.

"The Lord is already here," said Pace. "He has been working through these good people to bring dignity and honor to this child."

"You preach words of damnation, old man." He lifted the Bible above his head. "The Spirit has forsaken you and all the heathen who refuse to heed the commands of the Almighty."

Before Pace could reply, Fats McCauley spoke in a low rumble, the words erupting from deep inside his corpulent body. "Judge not lest ye yourself be judged. For the Lord knoweth the way of the righteous, but the way of the ungodly shall perish." With the last syllable, his face froze. His eyes never wavered from Leroy Jackson as he silently challenged the man to dispute him.

"Amen," said Pace.

Leroy Jackson looked away, unable to tolerate the weight of Fats McCauley's soul-piercing scrutiny. Through the doorway came Luke Coleman. He moved past his neighbor and self-proclaimed preacher as he led his wife Harriet by the arm. The young mother had draped a remnant of black lace across her head. The brown hair was pulled into a bun, and her dark eyes darted beneath the drooping veil, painfully searching each face for reassurance that her son was not lost to her.

She caught sight of the casket at the far end of the room. The profile of the child rose above the padded rim as if he lay suspended over a sea of white satin. Harriet Coleman drew back. Her legs crumpled. Luke tried to catch her, but she sank to the hardwood floor.

"My boy," she sobbed. "Why would God let him die? He didn't need to die." Her husband struggled to raise her to her feet. Pace took her other arm and together they managed to carry her to a folding chair that Wayne set up against the wall. The woman shut out all attempts to comfort her, only staring at the casket, her grief grown too deep for any physical expression.

"Are you expecting others?" I asked Luke Coleman.

"Some friends and neighbors. Leroy will say a few words before we all leave for Kentucky."

I nodded and patted the man on the arm. "I'll be close by to be of assistance." I gave a slight wave of my hand indicating we should withdraw. Fats McCauley was not watching for the signal. He was fascinated by the young mother and studied her as if she were the only person in the room.

"Travis," I whispered, then repeated more distinctly. There was no response.

"Travis, let's go," said Pace.

The big man nodded, but instead of following the Reverend, he crossed the room and knelt in front of Harriet Coleman, putting his bulk between her and the casket.

"You have a beautiful little boy. Nobody will take that memory away from you. Believe me."

Harriet Coleman reached out and touched Fats McCauley on the cheek. She rubbed her fingers across his tears.

"He is with Jesus, isn't he?"

"Yes. Yes, he is. And my Brenda is with Jesus too. Happy and whole in the shelter of His arms." He took a deep breath, then whispered so low that the rest of us strained to catch the words. "Too cold. It was too cold."

Fats McCauley got to his feet, looked back at the boy and walked out of the room without another word.

"I'm going to sit with Fats for a few minutes in the kitchen," said Pace.

I turned to Susan. "Would you mind helping me at the front door? Folks can put their coats in the hall closet."

About fifteen or twenty people came. Most were like the Colemans, poor, ill-clad, and terribly distraught by the tragedy. Like the Colemans and Leroy Jackson, they had migrated over from Kentucky. As the colony's spiritual leader, Jackson dealt with the mourners more as tribe members than as a congregation.

I was surprised at the one exception to this group of backwoods mountaineers. Fred Pryor, the Ridgemont Power and Electric executive, walked into the foyer wearing a tan cashmere overcoat.

Accompanying him was a lean man with oily black hair and the dark stubble of a well-past-five-o'clock shadow. He wore a wrinkled gray suit and would have been almost presentable if not for the scuffed brown shoes. I figured him for late-forties. He helped Pryor out of his coat while never taking his eyes off me. There was no chance I could mistake his expression as friendly. He was wary, like a dog protecting his turf.

"Mr. Clayton," said Pryor. "Sorry to meet again under such sad circumstances. And I gather there is still no word on Dallas Willard?"

I shook my head. Pryor turned to his companion.

"This is Odell Taylor. He is one of our foremen. I asked him to have the crew check the security gate at the head of the rail spur and walk the track."

I reached out to shake the man's hand, but instead Taylor laid Pryor's heavy coat across my forearm.

"Nothin'," he said. "We found nothin' because that Willard knows better than to set foot on our property."

Pryor quickly touched the man's wrist and interrupted him. "I know, Odell, but Mr. Clayton and the Sheriff are just doing their best to pursue every possibility. All of us hope the poor demented man is found alive. The loss of the…the…"

He faltered for a second, and Odell Taylor said, "Colemans' son."

"Yes, the loss of the Colemans' son is enough tragedy to deal with. We'd better go pay our respects."

Pryor eyed the visitation room as if studying the fairway before a golf shot. Then he and his "caddie" walked into the crowd. Susan took Pryor's coat from me and whispered, "Who's Mr. Personality and the Big Shot?"

"The Big Shot is Fred Pryor, the guy Tommy Lee and I met at Broad Creek. Mr. Personality is his foreman. He's helping his boss keep faces and names together. I'd just as soon he forget mine."

Susan and I stood at the doorway where we could be of assistance in case someone needed a restroom. Uncle Wayne stayed close to the young mother. She sat in her chair blankly staring ahead. People made short statements of condolence and then moved on to small circles of conversation.

Fred Pryor spent about ten minutes making small talk with folks he recognized from the construction site, but whose jobs kept them nameless. As I expected, Taylor positioned himself beside Pryor and cued each first name so that the boss could say hello and agree how terrible a tragedy it was and what good friends they were to come.

Then I saw Pryor look around the room and decide it was time for him to get to the purpose of his visit. He cleared his throat just loud enough to halt conversation around him. The silence rippled through the room as he walked over to the Colemans. He pulled a brown envelope from his inside pocket and handed it to Luke.

"We hope this can help in your hour of need."

Everyone watched intently, recognizing the standard pay envelope of Ridgemont Power and Electric. Luke opened the unsealed flap. He studied the enclosure without removing it, and then passed it to his wife. "Thank you, Mr. Pryor," he muttered, never lifting his eyes.

Harriet removed the check and held it between her splintered fingernails. She looked over its edge to the body of her son. Tears flushed her eyes and the check shook uncontrollably.

"A hundred dollars. A hundred dollars for the life of my Jimmy." Her face twisted, and the check fluttered to the floor.

The color rose in Fred Pryor's cheeks. Those were not the words of gratitude he expected. The woman had humiliated him. I knew he wanted to snatch up the check and storm out.

"It's an hour of need. Need and understanding," said Wayne. "We thank you for your thoughtfulness, Mr. Pryor." My uncle stood behind the sobbing woman and turned his gentle smile on the whole room, diffusing the tension. Wayne's sensitivity, like that of my father, was something you don't learn in embalming school. It was something I found difficult to express.

Fred Pryor pushed the bile back in his throat and managed to nod an acceptance of the compliment. Leroy Jackson knelt and picked up the check. As he raised it past Harriet Coleman, she reached out with the swiftness of a serpent, snared it from his hand and clutched it to her breast.

I felt a body bump against me, and I slid aside as Fats McCauley squeezed between me and the doorjamb. He made no apology as he stood staring into the room, his heavy face moving side to side as he searched for someone.

"Brenda," he said. "I want to tell the mother about my Brenda."

Only the rustle of clothing broke the silence as people turned to see who had spoken. Odell Taylor stepped forward as if challenging Fats to intrude farther.

A hand grabbed Fats firmly by the shoulder and pulled him back into the foyer. With strength beyond his physical appearance, Reverend Pace spun the obese man around.

"Not tonight, Travis." Pace put his face only inches away from the other man. "This is not the time. Right now we have to take care of the living." Pace looked at Susan and me. "Would you take him home?"

We got Fats' raincoat from the closet. He draped it over his shoulders like a cape and followed us out the rear of the funeral home and into the steady drizzle. We drove to his furniture store in the old section of Main Street. Gainesboro's small downtown had not yet been totally cannibalized by the shopping malls, but on this rainy Sunday night we encountered no one. The silence of the ghost town was invaded only by the whoosh of my tires on the wet pavement and the steady slap of the windshield wipers.

We stopped in front of the brick two-story building with "McCauley's Furniture" scripted across the plate glass window.

"We still live upstairs," he said softly. "Thank you."

He wedged himself out the curb-side door, and then he crossed in front of my headlights. I rolled down the window, wondering if he had left something at the funeral home.

"Can we talk tomorrow?" he whispered. He glanced over at Susan and spoke even softer. "Private?"

"Sure," I said. "I'll come by."

He reached in with a damp hand and gently patted my bandaged shoulder. Then he turned and lumbered into the store like a black bear retreating to his den.

"What was that all about?" asked Susan.

"I don't know."

"Something's hurting him. Who's Brenda?"

"His daughter," I said. "She died a long time ago, but she still haunts him."

Chapter 6

On Monday the hunt for Dallas Willard was smaller in scale since most of the weekend volunteers held regular jobs and Tommy Lee had limited manpower. I planned to drop by the Sheriff's Department early and lend a hand in whatever way I could. I hoped that Reverend Pace and I would be paired together again. With the odds growing that we might be looking for Dallas' body, I preferred someone whose exuberance for the chase was not quite as overt as that displayed by Deputy Reece Hutchins. I'm sure Reece made a fine law officer, but most of my conversations with him during our search had revolved around his fantasies of how he would react to an ambush. Maybe he was just steadying his nerves, but he got on mine.

I was also unsettled by Fats' request to speak with me. Something was bothering him, and for some reason he wasn't comfortable discussing it in front of Susan. It could have merely been his old-school notion that there are some topics men should only talk about with other men. He certainly had seemed shocked by the idea of Reverend Pace having a female colleague. I suspected the terrible tragedy of little Jimmy Coleman's death lay beneath Fats' anxiety, and I decided I should see him before meeting Tommy Lee.

I had been six when Brenda McCauley was murdered. We had been in first grade together. A handyman who did odd jobs for Fats lured the trusting little girl into his car. Her body was found in a drainage ditch three days later. The killing cut our community to the quick. My classmates and I were sheltered from the grisly details, and only when I was much older did I learn she had been sodomized. The murderer died a week later in a shootout with police in north Georgia.

Losing a classmate when you're six makes a lasting impact. I couldn't see Fats without thinking of the lively red-haired girl who had once sat in the desk beside me. If I still felt some pain, what pain must Fats McCauley have had to endure every day of his life? Surely it was unbearable. Fats' wife left him on the first anniversary of their daughter's death, unable to separate her husband from the anguish of their loss. I thought about my father and his fading memory and thought at times it could be a blessing.

At ten till eight, most of the Main Street stores were still closed. Of course, P's Barbershop bustled with the usual crowd of Monday morning gossips who clustered around the central kerosene heater, drinking coffee, watching haircuts, and telling tall tales. It was the place to learn who did what to whom over the weekend.

McCauley's Furniture was three stores down from the barbershop. I parked at the curb and peered into the dim store front, but I couldn't see any activity. The "Drink Sundrop" open-for-business sign taped inside the front door announced Monday—Friday: eight-thirty to five. I guessed Fats would be up by now since the store should open in less than an hour.

I jiggled the door latch and wasn't surprised to find it locked. I banged on the window glass, but the anemic rattle did not sound as if it could be heard beyond the love seats and winged-back chairs visible in the morning sunlight.

I noticed no cars were parked at the curb. Fats' vehicle must have been kept in the rear alley. I cut through the walkway between McCauley's Furniture and Larson's Discount Drugs, dodging the boxes of trash set out by the druggist for Monday pickup. The furniture store had no exit along the side. At the rear, an old silver Buick sat snug against Fats' loading dock door. On the far side was a service entrance with an electric buzzer to signal a delivery. I had expected that. I didn't expect the broken windowpane above the doorknob. The sight of the jagged daggers of glass snapped me fully alert like no cup of coffee ever could.

I carefully reached for the inside latch, and swung the door open with my knee, leaving my good arm free should the intruder be waiting in the shadows. A floorboard creaked as I stepped across the threshold. It was the only sound other than my own breathing. I waited for my eyes to adjust. In the gloom, a packing crate became visible in the corner by the stairway to the second floor. Its lid had been pried off for a preliminary inspection of its contents. A crowbar dangled from the splintered edge where the nails had been ripped from the wood. I grabbed the flat end and balanced the cool iron in my hand. A swift swing would turn it into a lethal weapon, capable of breaking an arm or skull.

From the rear of the store, I could clearly see the silhouettes of furniture cluttered against the daylight of the front windows. The cash register at the counter appeared undisturbed. Perhaps the burglar, if he had indeed gotten inside, had fled before getting a chance to rifle the cash drawer. I decided to announce my presence in case an alarmed Fats McCauley was upstairs loading a shotgun.

"Mr. McCauley! Mr. McCauley, it's Barry Clayton." I kept the crowbar by my side and climbed the stairs, calling out with every step. I pushed open the door to the apartment and heard the sound of running water. Then I felt the wetness soak through my shoes. I crossed the small living room toward the hallway. My footsteps squished in the puddles that collected in the depressions of the hardwood floor. I found a wall switch and the overhead light illuminated the short corridor. Water flowed under the door at the end of the hall, its pink tinge offering an ominous explanation of why no one answered.

I slowly pushed the door open. In the dim light, I saw a shapeless mass quivering above the porcelain rim of the tub. I needed a few seconds to comprehend that I was staring at what once had been a human being.

The remains of Fats' head lay against the spigot, bobbing in its generated turbulence and floating just above the surface, while the rest of his body filled the tub. His flaccid mass was not round but layered in folds where the fat creased back on itself. The buoyant flesh rippled in macabre vibrations as the water swirled around the corpse and flowed over the tub's edge onto the floor.

"Oh, hell," I muttered. I saw the thick splotches of blood, hair, flesh, and brains splattered against the tile wall from the soap dish to the ceiling. A single discharged shotgun shell lay in the dry wash basin to my right. It was a number one buck Remington twelve gauge, the same kind of shell I saw ricochet off Martha Willard's casket.

"Don't disturb anything," ordered Tommy Lee. "I'll be right there."

I started to remind him I had worked in a police department, but I decided I'd probably say the same thing to anyone standing smack in the middle of a murder scene. I set the phone receiver back on the cradle, careful to hold it where I would not smudge any prints. There was nothing I could do for Fats. I took the few remaining minutes before the coming onslaught of law enforcement officials and media hounds to indulge my old police curiosity about the crime scene.

The writing desk in his bedroom was tidy. I had used the black rotary-dial phone I found squared in the back right corner. The goose-necked lamp was on the left. A plain white message pad lay in the center of the desk. Several sheets had been torn off leaving a red-gummed rim of adhesive binding sticking a quarter inch above the top sheet. Nothing was written on the pad, although I noticed an imprint from the previous notation—"Barry Clayton weather."

Just to the side of the desk was a wire-mesh waste basket, its bottom covered with wadded note sheets. I wondered if the one bearing my name was among them. On the floor next to the waste basket lay a retractable ball-point pen with "McCauley's Furniture" gilded on the blue plastic barrel. The tip was clicked in position for writing.

Everything else in the sparsely furnished room seemed in order. The clothes I had seen Fats wearing yesterday were piled in the desk chair. The single bed was made, but the spread had been neatly folded back from the pillow. A closed black Bible rested on the crisp white pillowcase.

I returned to the hall and opened the door across from Fats' bedroom. Inside, it was as dark as if night had suddenly fallen on that half of the apartment. I fumbled along the wall until I found the face plate through my handkerchief. I flipped up the stubby switch.

In the light, I found myself staring nearly twenty-five years into the past. Against the far wall was a single bed covered with a faded peach spread. The oversized white pillow provided support for a collection of cherished stuffed animals: a teddy bear, a purple frog, a Raggedy Ann and Raggedy Andy. Stacked on the nightstand were *My First Speller* and *My First Math*, school books that had never been returned. Everything was waiting for the touch of a little hand that would never come. Fats had turned the room into a shrine.

"This changes everything." Tommy Lee slowly twirled the silver pen in his hand. Around it rotated the discharged shotgun shell he had carefully lifted from the sink. The two of us stood in the bathroom, momentarily oblivious to the floating corpse behind us. We stared at the evidence both of us saw linking Dallas Willard to another murder.

"I've got my search teams spread out through the hills, and he walks into town and shoots an innocent man in the bathtub."

"What's the motive?" I asked.

"I'll be damned if I can see it. Maybe there isn't one. Maybe he's just nuts. Maybe this didn't come from Dallas' shotgun and I'm the one who's nuts. Or simply the last to learn that Remington number one buckshot is the new weapon of choice. Well, I'll run down Main Street wearing only my holster if the firing pin mark on this shell doesn't match those from the cemetery." He slipped the shell into a plastic evidence sleeve. "If it's Dallas, and if there is no logical motive, then every citizen in this county is a potential victim."

"Let me show you something else," I said. I took Tommy Lee into Fats' bedroom and pointed to the notepad on the desk. "Looks like Fats or somebody wrote down my name and the word weather. Maybe the sheet is in the trash."

"Weather?"

"It was raining last night. Could be two separate thoughts."

"The state mobile crime lab is on the way. I want them going over the apartment before we remove the body. I'll tell them to look out for anything that might have come off this pad. No way to know if he wrote it last night or last week."

"Last night he asked to speak to me. Maybe I was on today's To-Do List."

"Speak to you about what?" asked Tommy Lee.

"I don't know. He was upset by the death of that little boy. Just look in his daughter's room if you want a glimpse of Fats' private hell."

"Listen, Barry. I want you to watch your back. Dallas tried to kill you once. He may now have your name in the same pocket as his shotgun shells. Motive or not, he has moved beyond killing his immediate family."

"And there has got to be a connection," I said. "It must be about the land. Was Fats trying to buy it from Dallas' brother and sister?"

"Fats never went out of town. You think he could tote his bulk up and down the side of a mountain?"

"I meant as an investment."

"Hell, Barry, to be honest I haven't had two minutes to worry about the land."

"Then no one talked to Linda Trine?" I asked. "Remember Alex Soles told me she observed Dallas ranting at the migrant workers."

The sheriff shook his head. "One of those meant-to-do things. Since we knew Dallas pulled the trigger, I didn't waste time trying to build a case against him when the priority was to bring him in. Want to do us both a favor?"

"Sure."

"Go see Linda Trine for me. And see if she knows anything about this." He pulled a folded sheet of common white typing paper out of his chest pocket and smoothed the creases until it lay flat on the desk. An oval had been sketched with what looked like three bands drawn across it. A lopsided sandwich. The top layer was labeled L.W. and bottom layer, N.J. The initials F.W. were imprinted on the middle one. Martha Willard's signature was in the upper right-hand corner of the page, and beneath it was the date April 25th.

"Here is a photocopy of what I found on Dallas' kitchen table when I searched the cabin after the shooting. I figure this is a map. If all the Willard property is deeded in Martha's name, then this may be how she wanted it portioned up. N.J. is Norma Jean, and L.W. is Lee Willard. F.W. must be some other relative, meaning Dallas Willard got shut out completely. Must have driven him over the edge and he killed the other two."

"Then why wasn't he mad at his grandmother?" I asked. "She drew up the map, but Dallas made it a point for me to tell her he loved her when I met up with her in heaven. That's the reason he shot me."

"Yeah," said Tommy Lee. "I couldn't quite square that part either. Thought maybe you'd have some ideas."

I examined the sheet of paper. It didn't look like a legal document, more an illustration of intentions. The April date corresponded to the time Norma Jean had prepaid Martha's funeral. It was logical that if Norma Jean and Martha were making final burial arrangements, they would also update or complete a will. Perhaps all the grandchildren had received such a drawing, and somewhere an attorney would have the proper documents to turn this sketch into a surveyed and registered inheritance.

Why was Dallas excluded? And who was F.W.? Then the answer came to me. "This is Dallas," I said, pointing to the middle layer. "Remember I told you Grandma Martha had started calling him Francis."

"Oh, yeah, Saint Francis of Assisi because he talked to the animals." He shook his head. "What a family. How could she possibly be considered to be of sound mind and then will part of her land to Saint Francis?"

"Norma Jean probably went to the attorney with her. It's not considered irrational to bequeath your estate to your nearest of kin. I'm sure the official paperwork does not include the name Francis."

"Well, knowing the Willard property like I do," said Tommy Lee, "it makes sense. That center section is the highest ground, and it's the prettiest. Couple of bold streams flow off of it. I could see Dallas moving up there."

"Nobody lives on this property now?" I asked.

"You know mountaineers own land they set aside for hunting," he explained. "They settled in the valleys and surrounded themselves with ample forest for both privacy and game. It's only in the last fifteen years that developers have eyed these ridges as prized real estate. I'd say Martha Willard was just stubborn enough to hold onto her tract."

"But the grandchildren may have seen it differently," I said. "That's cause enough for a feud."

"Yep. Look into it while I try to make some sense of the madness here."

"Can I take this?" I asked, reaching for the map.

"It's yours. The original is in the case file and this copy sure as hell ain't doing me any good stuck in my pocket."

Chapter 7

Linda Trine's office was located in the limbo land between Gainesboro's commercial district and the more popular Sky High Mall several miles out at the interstate where the incoming tourists first exited. The stretch of highway included light industrial offices, fast-food franchises, and an assortment of gasoline and convenience stations.

The Appalachian Relief Center was not a center at all, but rather a loose network of charity organizations with the common purpose of serving mountain families in need. A.R.C. offices were scattered throughout the mountain cities of the Carolinas, Tennessee, Virginia, West Virginia, and Kentucky. Linda Trine had taken what twenty-five years ago had been her church social service committee and through hard work and unwavering dedication unified relief efforts into a nationally recognized operation. She accomplished all of it without creating proliferating bureaucracy and escalating overhead.

A.R.C. shared a metal warehouse building with a dog-grooming business. I drove past the first entrance. It led into the front lot where women parked their cars and carried their precious canines in for the absurd beautifications performed by the Purple Velvet Poodle Parlor. The second drive looped around the backside of the building to the offices and warehouse that dispensed food, blankets, and clothing to a segment of humanity upon which life had lavished only hard times.

The waiting room was furnished in the ever popular curbside-recyclable motif consisting of a lumpy sofa, three straight-backed chairs, and a recliner permanently jammed in the extended position. The furniture was peopled with two lean-faced women, four shaggy children, and a grizzled man, aged somewhere between fifty and seventy, who sat beneath the THANK YOU FOR NOT SMOKING poster, a cigarette dangling between his lips. They all waited in impoverished silence.

I walked over to the receptionist who, giving me little more than a cursory glance at the hand protruding from my stomach, shoved a form across the counter, turned back to her filing and said, "Fill it out and report the date of your last visit if known."

"Sorry," I said, "I'm Barry Clayton, and I'm here to speak to Linda Trine about Dallas Willard."

The woman gave me her full attention. Everyone knew about Dallas Willard.

"Mr. Clayton?" She questioned if she had repeated my name correctly. I nodded reassurance. "Let me ring her for you." After a brief word on the phone, she directed me to the back door. The hallway beyond fed four small offices before flowing out into the storage warehouse.

Linda Trine stuck her beaming face out of the last door on the left. "Barry, I heard you were in season. Remind me never to stand beside you at a funeral." She ushered me into her office, picked up a stack of files from the seat of a chair, dumped them on the floor, and bade me sit down. Organized chaos surrounded us. In addition to the piles of paper on the floor and desk, the walls were adorned with Post-It notes proclaiming a variety of names, dates, and phone numbers.

Linda pulled a wooden swivel chair from behind the desk so that she wouldn't have to stare over the mountainous mess. She was what folks in the country call a big-boned, healthy gal, probably pushing six feet in height and sixty years in age. We crossed paths occasionally if I was conducting a funeral for one of her clients. She was always good to attend and be of comfort to the family. Linda sported a no-nonsense attitude, and I knew whatever I asked her, she would give me a straight answer. In keeping with that trait, her welcoming humor vanished and her brow furrowed with undiluted concern.

"How can I help?" she asked, getting straight to the purpose of my visit.

"Dallas Willard," I said. "This hasn't been made public yet, but it looks like he killed Fats McCauley last night."

"Good God," she exclaimed. "You sure?"

"Evidence needs to be checked, but I'd say the odds are Dallas walked into town and killed Fats in his apartment. We have no idea why."

"Have you talked to Alex Soles?"

"He said you told him Dallas acted strangely."

"Did he say I thought Dallas needed help?"

"Yes. Alex came to me in the hospital tremendously upset that he hadn't followed up on your request."

"He never saw Dallas? I can't believe it. I was very specific about it." Her amazement turned to visible anger.

"What made you speak to Alex?" I asked.

"I've known Dallas since he was four. He's always been shy and reserved. Everyone knew he wasn't quite normal, but he'd never been violent. So, it was completely out of character when Miguel Rodriguez complained about him."

"Who's Miguel Rodriguez?"

"Oversees the migrant camps. He's an investigator for the wage and hour division of the U.S. Department of Labor. Compliance officer is the old term. He works with migrant farm laborers from Florida to Virginia. He makes inspections throughout the growing season, not only regarding wage payments but also living conditions."

"How'd Rodriguez cross paths with Dallas?"

"It seems a few months ago Dallas verbally harassed a bus load of workers unloading at the Bennetts Creek camp that borders the Willard property. Stood off on the side of the road shouting for their destruction. 'Set one foot on my land and God Almighty will consume you with hellfire.' Miguel said it was stuff like that. Most of the workers are Hispanic and speak little English, but it still unnerved them to see Dallas ranting and raving. Miguel was there that day."

"Did he talk to Dallas?" I asked.

"He tried, but Dallas turned his epithets on Miguel, then drove off in his pickup. I swung by the next afternoon when the bus brought the workers from the fields. Dallas was standing by the road, like a prophet out of the wilderness, yelling as they got off and went to their shanties."

"Did you talk to him?"

"Just for a few minutes. He knew me well enough to calm down. Told me they were plotting to take his land and that he would die first. I tried to get through to him that these were simple people with no power to do anything. He just looked at me for a few seconds, then he whispered more to himself than to me, 'Yes, the power controls them and they don't know it.' With that cryptic pronouncement, he left. Barry, Dallas seemed psychotic, and that was my big concern. I telephoned Alex Soles. He said Dallas wasn't his patient, but that he was part of an Alzheimer's support group. Alex said he would speak with him."

"Well, that explains why Alex was so upset when he saw me at the hospital."

"And since Dallas never came back to the camps, I thought everything was under control."

"Why would he think the migrants wanted his land?" I asked.

"Because there is a proposal to build a central migrant facility. It grew out of a government study that concluded better care and living conditions could be provided if everything in the county were consolidated at one location. Dallas must have gotten wind of it and thought they wanted the family property. Maybe he was actually approached, or he heard some of the farmers discussing it. That's all I know,

Barry, and I've only learned that since I spoke to Dallas. It still doesn't explain why he'd murder his own family, or why he tried to kill you."

I pulled the map from my pocket. "Did he show you this? It's a rough drawing of how Martha Willard's property could be divided."

Linda studied it for a few seconds, and then shook her head. "Have you talked to Carl Romeo?"

"No. How is he involved?" The Gainesboro attorney had drawn up my parents' wills.

"Evidently he handled Martha Willard's estate. Dallas said he'd take Carl a paper to stop them."

"This paper?"

"I don't know. Maybe you ought to drop by and see him."

As soon as I got in my Jeep, I called the law office of Carl Romeo and was told Mr. Romeo was just on his way to a luncheon meeting.

"This is Barry Clayton," I said. "I need to speak to him for one minute."

After a few seconds of silence, Carl's voice broke through. "My God, Barry, how are you?"

"All things considered, I'm fine. But I need to talk to you. When are you out of your luncheon meeting?"

"What luncheon meeting?" he said, and then he laughed. "That was just Ruth making sure I get lunch. Plus she wants my clients to think I'm always headed for some power rendezvous. I was running a few errands and grabbing a bite at a drive-through."

"Sit tight and I'll bring lunch to you. My treat. You can have anything on the Cardinal Cafe menu."

Sitting at his conference table, I wondered if Carl Romeo and Linda Trine had taken the same office organization seminar. File folders had to be swept to either side to clear a spot for our roast beef sandwiches and onion rings. Carl declined the jumbo root beer I brought him and retrieved a low-cal soda from the mini-refrigerator in the corner.

"The wife's got me on a diet," he remarked, just before popping an onion ring in his mouth and licking the grease traces off his fingers. It crossed his mind that I no longer had a wife to worry about my waistline, and he asked, "You got someone to help you, Barry? Must be a bitch tying your shoes with one hand."

"The secret is to never take them off."

He laughed. "And I thought it was the food that smelled funny."

Carl was first-generation local. For a lawyer that was a good status to claim. It meant your family hadn't been around long enough for you to know everybody's business, but you had grown up under the eyes of the old-timers. You weren't an outsider, or worse, a freshly transplanted Yankee. Carl's dad had been a doctor who moved down from New Jersey, setting up practice immediately out of residency. When your name ends in a vowel, you're a Yankee: if you're also one of ten Catholics in the county, you stick out. Getting established forty years ago had been tough, but Doc Romeo pulled enough emergency room duty and helped enough hurting folks who didn't care where he moved from or what he believed in as long as he could ease their pain, that local folks were soon anxious to pass the word that he was just as good as a normal person.

Carl was several years older than me, falling on the plus or minus side of forty. He had a high forehead accentuated by an ever-receding hairline. Round, gold-framed glasses perched halfway down his nose, and he was perpetually rubbing his hand across a brown mustache that was not only salted with gray but now liberally peppered with crumbs of fried onion rings. The extra chin spreading over the knot in his tie had probably prompted his wife's dietary demands.

He had the reputation for being a crackerjack attorney. If I knew only one thing, it was that the Willard family had done well to enlist his aid.

Carl swallowed the last morsel of sandwich and swept the wrappings into a wastebasket. He completed my one-armed efforts to clean my own mess, and then sat back down and leaned across the table. "Now, Barry, what specifically can I do for you?"

"First, I need to tell you some bad news."

He sat up straight, backing away as if what I was about to say could physically touch him.

"What? Has Dallas been killed?"

"No. I gather you've been in the office all morning because I'm sure it's public knowledge by now. Last night Fats McCauley was killed in his apartment by a shotgun. Dallas Willard is the prime suspect."

"Fats McCauley?" He sighed. "What has gotten into that boy?"

"I'm hoping you can tell me. I'm trying to help run down some loose ends for Sheriff Tommy Lee Wadkins, and as you can guess, I've got a personal interest. I understand you're handling the Willard estate."

He shook his head as if I had just asked him to fix the national debt.

"I wish I'd never heard the name Willard."

"Why's that?"

"Because they've been nothing but trouble."

"Was it just bad luck they came to you?" I asked.

The length of Carl's silence told me the Willards had been more than walk-in clientele. It must be genetic that people who become lawyers cannot begin a conversation without weighing the implications of every word. When at last he reached some comfort with how to proceed, he cleared his throat and spoke in a tone that made me feel like I was taking his deposition.

"First of all, let me state that to the best of my knowledge everything regarding the Willards that I've seen has been handled on the up and up. I say that because some of the procedures may seem a little complex, but each requested action was well within the law.

"About ten years ago, a client came to me and asked for a favor. Over the years he had provided me with a hefty sum of legal fees, so, naturally I lent a receptive ear. His proposition concerned the Willard property. He was interested in acquiring it, but smart enough to know you didn't just walk in on Martha Willard and make her an offer. Selling family land would be traumatic. After all, what would all the dead ancestors think? And land values had skyrocketed during Martha's lifetime. The capital gains tax would be obscene. Martha would sooner give money to the devil than to the IRS.

"My client figured a way around these obstacles, and he wanted me to start the ball rolling by approaching Pastor Stinnett."

"Martha's preacher?" I interrupted. "You were going to get him to make Martha sell her land?"

Carl broke out in one of those "you're-going-to-love-this" grins. "He was going to get Martha to give away the land. She would gift the land to Crab Apple Valley Baptist Church. I would be responsible for setting up a trust, a charitable remainder trust to be exact. The charitable trust would receive the property, sell it avoiding the taxes, and then begin legally paying Martha an income based on the interest earnings of the trust. She could start reaping cash from an asset that was currently providing nothing.

"But what my client thought would really capture Martha's support was the creation of the trust itself, The Martha Willard Trust, because when she died, all the money left in it would revert to the church."

"How much?" I asked.

"Three hundred thousand back then. Enough to get Preacher Stinnett's attention. That's a hell of a lot of collection plates."

"That's fine for him," I said, "but wasn't Martha cheating her heirs?"

"Her son Robbie had died, and the three grandchildren, Norma Jean, Lee, and Dallas were the only immediate family. At that time Martha was a spry sixty and never sick a day in her life. Her Alzheimer's had not yet materialized. That's where Archie Donovan came into the picture."

"The insurance agent?"

"Yes, we had figured in a premium that Martha would pay out of her new income. It would purchase a three hundred thousand dollar policy on her life with the grandchildren as beneficiaries. That would repay them the money that went to the church. Everybody wins but the IRS."

"Obviously something went wrong. Was it just too complicated for everyone to understand?"

"No, I went to see Preacher Stinnett and he jumped on the idea like a robin on a junebug. He took me with him to see Martha right away, and he suggested I let him do the talking." Carl shook his head and laughed as he recalled the meeting. "Preacher Stinnett was amazing. He presented it as if it were his idea. No, it was more of a dream he had. While he slept, God spoke to him saying that the church would always be freshly painted, that the cemetery would overflow with flowers, that the ladies' quilting circle of which Martha was a life-long member would never want for supplies. Preacher Stinnett said he asked, 'How can this be, Lord? We are a congregation rich in faith but poor in worldly goods.' And the Lord spoke majestically the words, 'My beloved servant Martha Willard can provide.' And then Stinnett said there appeared a sheaf of papers on which was written the name Carl Romeo. 'So, I sought him out and discovered he was a wise attorney and a God-fearing man who knew the Lord's will. He has shown me how those who sow unto God will themselves reap abundantly.' The Preacher turned to me, and I realized that was my introduction."

"Laid it on kind of thick, didn't he," I said.

"I must have looked like a fool, sitting there in a doily-covered armchair with my mouth hanging open. 'Go ahead, Mr. Romeo,' he prompted. 'Show her the diagrams, especially the one that gives the money to the Lord instead of the tax man.'

"I managed to compose myself and drew a simple flow chart of how things would work. Martha followed pretty well and seemed genuinely interested. She asked a few questions, mainly about the insurance and could her own doctor perform the required physical. Then she announced she would pray about it and then have us return for a family meeting."

"With her and her grandchildren?"

"Yes, I got the feeling if they had no serious objections Martha would fulfill Preacher Stinnett's prophecy. A week later I was back in her small living room with my charts. Norma Jean and Lee were all for it. They had no attachment to the land, and they liked the idea that Martha had more money coming in. I'm sure their tax-free three hundred thousand dollar inheritance didn't hurt either."

"Dallas was different," I said.

"Dallas fell apart. It was awful. At first he got angry. Then he started crying. Wailing is more like it. He and his father had hunted on that land, and his dad had promised some day the ridge would be his. At sixteen, he was the youngest. His father died when he was fourteen. The mother had died when Dallas was only seven, leaving him to the maternal care of Grandma Martha. He was the baby of the family by more than five years and still held that place in his grandmother's heart.

"Well, his pathetic reaction turned Martha's mind against the plan. She wouldn't contradict Dallas' wishes. The others wanted her to give two-thirds of the land, carving out the section Dallas wanted. Preacher Stinnett looked at me, but I shook my head no. My client would not agree to buy property with the center gutted out of it. I rolled up my papers and left the room. There was nothing I could do, and frankly, the tension between Dallas and his brother and sister bordered on open confrontation. Perhaps the seeds of murder were sown that day."

"Perhaps," I agreed. I also recalled Preacher Stinnett's glare of disapproval when Dallas arrived at the graveside. He knew because of Dallas he was also burying three hundred thousand. "But you've seen the family since then?"

"Yes. About six months ago, Norma Jean brought Martha in to have her will drawn. Her general health was failing rapidly, but although her Alzheimer's was beginning to make an impact, Martha remembered me and said she knew I had only been trying to help. Norma Jean said her grandmother wanted the land to come to them intact, with equal ownership of the whole parcel."

"Not carving it up," I said. "Giving Dallas the ridge section."

"No, Norma Jean was very specific on that point."

I handed him the map from Dallas Willard's cabin. "Not like this?" I asked.

"No," said Carl. "You know Ruth said Dallas brought something like this by the office the day after Martha died. I was out of town. She told him it was not the way the estate would be settled, that Martha had directed that the land be held in common and that all the paperwork had been legally executed."

"So, what if someone wanted to buy the whole parcel and Dallas still didn't want to sell?"

"Simple majority vote of the owners."

"Did Dallas know that?"

"I assumed he did. But, given what happened the last time they tried to sell, his brother and sister could have intentionally kept him in the dark until Martha died."

"And then voted two to one against him. I understand both the power company and a migrant project are interested in the property, and it's probably worth more than three hundred thousand today."

"I wouldn't want to speculate," said Carl. "But you're right about the vote, although this document may have given Dallas a case."

I patted my bandaged shoulder. "Carl, I think it's safe to say he settled out of court."

Chapter 8

I traveled several miles outside of town and up from the valley floor to meet Tommy Lee at a local dive called Clyde's Roadside. Normally a five-minute trip, the drive took twenty because autumn tourists were as thick on the roads as—I could just hear my grandmother's voice—"ugly on a hog." She had said it in such a variety of contexts that it became a family expression for unwanted abundance.

The spectacular foliage of October kept a large number of Florida retirees in the western North Carolina mountains in unwanted abundance. And even a backwoods route did not avoid the perpetual parade of Cadillacs, Lincolns, and Buicks that crept along the winding two-lane blacktop, slowing at every break in the trees in hopes of a glimpse of some yet undiscovered panorama. My Jeep Cherokee wove through the maze as fast as the serpentine road would allow me to pass.

"Hello, sir, my name is Lindsay and did you see our specials board?" were words I would not hear inside the putrid green cinder block building of Clyde's Roadside. On the other hand, the Floridian drivers would definitely not be slowing down or stopping for this local color. At Clyde's the vehicle of choice, the pickup truck, outnumbered the cars two to one. I counted eight trucks, four cars, no out-of-state license plates, and no empty parking spaces in front.

I pulled around to the side. The site for Clyde's Roadside had been gouged out of the mountain, and a wall of dirt rose more than twenty feet above the parking lot. Naked ends of roots dangled where they had been mutilated and exposed by an earthmover's blade. Overhead, several pines at the edge of the man-made cliff leaned like green Towers of Pisa, waiting only for a windy push to topple them. Tommy Lee was parked in the V of double-stacked railroad ties which served as a make-shift dam against the torrents of water that would cascade down the slope during a heavy rain. I parked alongside him.

"Does this qualify as a rendezvous rather than a meeting?" I asked.

"My office is crawling with press. Hide at Clyde's is our safest bet if we want to talk undisturbed."

As we walked around the windowless exterior, I heard the bass notes of "Stand By Your Man" vibrate through the walls.

"At least they've got good music," I said.

"There are four copies of that song on the jukebox because they keep wearing out."

"They ought to get it on CD."

"Those are CDs," he said, and pushed the door open.

I was immediately hit by the smell of beer and peanuts.

"After you," he said.

As I suspected, someone named Lindsay was not there to ask if we preferred non-smoking. Instead, a soft gray haze flattened into a single layer and hung just below the rough-hewn ceiling planks. Neon American beer signs glowed beneath it. I would not be ordering a Newcastle Brown. As my eyes adjusted to the dimness, I spied the centerpiece behind the bar—a double-barrel shotgun which made Tommy Lee's brand of law enforcement unnecessary except for those occasional arguments which might spill out into the parking lot.

The patrons mostly drew from construction workers end-ing the day with a couple of brews, the unemployed who could afford Clyde's posted no-credit policy, and those mountain folk who tired of drinking corn liquor alone. About half the tables were filled, not with individuals, but with clusters of drinkers laughing or arguing to pass the time between swallows.

A distinct drop in the level of conversation started at the tables closest to the door and swept back across the room. Tammy Wynette's voice seemed to swell louder as the competition faded. Heads turned to the door to see what intrusion had broken the afternoon rituals. Tommy Lee just smiled and nodded his head with an unspoken "Howdy, boys." He walked over to the bar and ordered a draft of Bud for me and a Diet Coke for himself.

"Guess this means you're on-duty, Sheriff," said the skinny, gray-bearded barkeeper. He slid a dirt-spotted mug of foam across the chipped Formica surface to me and an unopened aluminum can to Tommy Lee.

"Just visiting, Clyde, if that's what you mean." He popped the top, took a deep pull on the soda and turned around to survey the crowd. "We'll start a tab and camp at a back table if that's all right with you."

"Sure. Take the one under the ugly guy in the corner."

As we crunched across discarded peanut shells, the men returned to their conversations. A few said hello, and one guy with a smile sporting broken and missing teeth that looked like the keys of a basement piano loudly asked for Tommy Lee's autograph. We knew why when we saw the election poster hanging over the table Clyde so graciously offered.

"At least they didn't deface it," I said.

"Probably afraid they'd improve my looks."

We sat down. Tommy Lee grabbed a handful of peanuts from the bucket on the table, crushed them in his fist, and started sorting through the hulls.

"What did you find out?" he asked.

I gave him my report on Linda Trine and Carl Romeo.

"Sounds like the motive is pretty clear," said Tommy Lee. "When Grandma Willard died, Dallas found out Norma Jean and Lee planned to cheat him out of his inheritance."

"Cheat him out of the land," I said. "He'd get his share of the money."

"Money doesn't mean squat to Dallas. You don't have to be crazy to want revenge when the thing you love most is being stolen from you."

"You think Dallas is sane?" I asked.

"No, I didn't say that. I think the boy has mental problems. Alex Soles says he's paranoid/schizophrenic. Little late with his diagnosis to do us any good. But just because Dallas was paranoid doesn't mean someone wasn't out to get him. And now he's lost all hope."

"What do you mean?"

"He can't inherit what he stands to gain through murder. His only motive was revenge—killing his brother and sister wouldn't get him the land."

"How do you know he knew that?" I asked. "He might be crazy enough not to understand the consequences of his actions and think he'll keep the property."

Tommy Lee stared at me for a few seconds. "You know, you just earned yourself another Bud. For that matter, who else stood to gain if Dallas killed his brother and sister?"

"Carl Romeo said Martha's grandchildren were the end of the line. He's going to do a check for any legal heirs the state would recognize, but the property will probably go to auction."

"A gift to the developers," growled Tommy Lee. "Unless Carl Romeo finds an heir." He thought for a second. "I wonder if that's an angle that ties Fats McCauley in somehow." He took the final swallow from his Coke can, but before he could say anything more, a noise invaded the bar like a hundred chain saws swirling around the building.

All other sounds stopped except for Tammy Wynette and the encircling roar from outside.

"Bikers," said Tommy Lee.

The throaty rumble told me the motorcycles were not luxurious Honda Gold Wings ridden by retired couples—

Cadillacs without doors. These had to be Harleys. In quick succession, four engines died.

The door to Clyde's Roadside swung inward, spilling the brilliance of the afternoon sun around the four silhouettes of the men who entered. The jangle of chains carried across the smoke-filled air. If I closed my eyes, it might have been the sound of spurs in a saloon. One of the men leaned over the bar and spoke to Clyde. The owner pointed at us.

"Oh, no," muttered Tommy Lee. He slid back slightly in his chair, ready to get to his feet.

I looked for a back door. There wasn't one. The largest of the bikers headed toward us with his comrades trailing behind. Men at other tables stared at us, knowing we were the gang's destination.

Sheriff Tommy Lee Wadkins smiled and spoke out of the corner of his mouth. "Cover me."

"Cover you?" My voice cracked through wilted vocal chords. "I'm a damn undertaker. The only thing I can cover you with is dirt."

They were close enough for me to hear the hobnails of their boots scraping across the floor's rough planks. The leader must have been somewhere between six and eight feet tall.

Tommy Lee whispered, "Then get ready to dig our way out of here."

The smell of the man's sweat reached us first. He stopped in front of Tommy Lee. The others fanned around us, sealing our corner table as tightly as a tomb. The quartet from hell sported heavy black leather jackets decorated with studs and chain links. The curly red-haired man closest to me had the tip of a letter B showing on his neck. I could guarantee the tattoo didn't say "Born to eat quiche."

"Saw your car, Sheriff. I've been looking for you. I hear you been spreading lies about me." The leader split his lips just enough to show he had fewer teeth than cards in a poker hand. His shoulder-length black hair was pulled back with a red bandanna, and a nut and bolt pierced his ear. Ugly on a hog took on a double meaning.

"What if I am? What are you going to do about it, Jack?"

I stared at Tommy Lee like he'd turned into a stranger. If he wanted to get the crap beat out of him, fine. I'd had my stay in the hospital this month. Let Tammy Wynette stand by him.

The man called Jack turned to me. A hollow whistle sounded as he sucked in air. "He a friend of yours?" he asked me.

"Look," I said. "I'm only an undertaker and I don't need any more business."

Big Jack looked at me for a second, and then started laughing. His cronies joined in. They stepped aside and let Clyde set a tray of six bottles of long-necked Bud on the table. Jack slapped me on the back. "That's a good one," he said, and then he shook Tommy Lee's hand. "I got the job, Sheriff. Maintenance foreman said you put in a good word."

"I know you can live up to it."

Each of the bikers grabbed a beer. Jack tipped it to Tommy Lee and then to the poster on the wall. "Thanks. Now how many times can we vote?"

Tommy Lee picked up a beer bottle and clinked it down the line. "Four. But only once each."

The bikers took their beers, their leather, their chains, and my fear to the next table.

"You bastard," I whispered.

"Me?" he laughed. "My opponent Bob Cain should have a friend like you. I thought you were going to pass out."

"Who is that guy?" I asked.

"Jack Andrews. I busted him a couple years ago for drug dealing. Small time. He pulled a light sentence and is on parole. Hell of a mechanic. I got him a job in Asheville working on police cars. Figure the more he's around cops, the more he'll like them. Maybe he'll stay straight. You do what you can." He looked at his watch. "Time to go off-duty," he said, and took a swig of the Bud.

I pushed my empty mug aside and grabbed the remaining bottle. "You do what you can," I agreed, and clinked his beer.

"Well now. Isn't this a sight."

I looked up to see a beefy man standing at our table. He wore a blue nylon jacket, and his white hair was buzz-cut to within a quarter-inch of his scalp. The smirk on his face begged to be wiped off.

He raised his voice above the din. "I saw your car in the parking lot and thought maybe you were actually making an arrest. But, no, a killer is running rampant through the county and our sheriff sits boozing it up in a bar."

Again, the room fell silent. Even Tammy Wynette was between encores.

"Come on, Cain," said Tommy Lee. "Why don't you take your hot air someplace else? We're having a meeting."

Bob Cain. Now I recognized him from his campaign posters. He didn't look the same without an American flag behind him.

"Having a meeting? Looks to me like you're having a drink." He glanced around the bar, expecting someone to laugh. No one did.

"Have you met Barry Clayton?" asked Tommy Lee. "He's a former police officer from Charlotte, and he was shot by Dallas Willard. He's consulting with me because unlike you I don't claim to know it all."

Cain's face reddened. "You need more help than he can give you."

"You heard the sheriff. Park your lip someplace else." Jack Andrews slid back from his table and stared at Cain.

"Butt out," said Cain. "When I'm sheriff, you and your pals will have to find some other county to stink up."

Cain may have been a security consultant, but he certainly didn't seem to think much about his own. Out of the corner of my eye, I saw Tommy Lee tense. The way things were headed he was going to have to keep his opponent from getting his ass stomped.

"You hear that boys," said Jack. "This gentleman thinks we stink." Jack stood up. Although Cain probably topped six-foot-two, the biker had a good three inches on him. "You know what I think?"

"Can you think?" asked Cain.

"Man, you got a mouth that just won't quit, don't you? I think when your momma was pregnant, a fart got in with the baby. The baby died and the fart lived. We do take baths, but you're gonna stink every day of your life."

The room erupted in laughter. Cain went from red to purple. His right fist came up from his side in a haymaker punch that caught Jack full force on the corner of his mouth. Jack's head barely moved under the blow, but a trickle of blood streamed down his chin. Cain froze, waiting for a response.

"I'd call that an assault, Sheriff," said Jack calmly. "Wouldn't you?"

"Yep, I would," replied Tommy Lee.

Before anyone could blink, Tommy Lee leaped from his chair and snapped a cuff on Cain's right wrist. The man turned to struggle, and Tommy Lee kicked him behind the knee, sending him face first into the peanut shells on the floor. The sheriff straddled his buttocks like Cain was a ride in the penny arcade, yanked Cain's left arm behind his back and cracked the other cuff across the left wrist. He grabbed the stainless steel bracelets and lifted Cain to his feet. He spun his hapless opponent around to face him. Ignoring the blood gushing from Cain's nose and mouth, Tommy Lee stared into his face, "You're under arrest."

For a few seconds, only the sound of a Nikon motor-drive could be heard. From a dark corner of the room, a young woman had stepped forward. She had a reporter's notepad tucked under her arm and a furiously flashing camera in her hands. Evidently, she'd been the one hiding in Clyde's the whole time.

"I'll read you your rights in the car," said Tommy Lee.

"You know you just got your department in one helluva law suit," said Cain. He turned his bloody face to the reporter's camera as it continued to snap off shots. "I'm suing for excessive use of force."

Tommy Lee shrugged off the threat. "You'll get your phone call and I'll ask Judge Wood to authorize releasing you on your own recognizance. I'm not making this personal, Cain. You'll get the same treatment as anybody else who breaks the law."

"You wouldn't know the law if it bit you in the ass."

Tommy Lee turned to Jack. "Thanks for taking the punch. I'll need a statement."

"You got it," said Jack. "I'll be down to press charges later. He's not worth interrupting my beer."

Tommy Lee pushed Cain ahead of him to the patrol car and locked him in the back seat. He picked up the mike and told the dispatcher he was bringing in a prisoner.

"Ten-four. And Sheriff, we've had a call about a poisoning," said the dispatcher.

"Didn't you call poison control?" He barked the question into the microphone.

"Negative. The victim is a horse."

"A what?"

"A horse. You know. Trigger. Hi, Ho, Silver."

"God-damn-it! I've got a killer on the loose and my political opponent in handcuffs. I'm not interested in a dead horse."

The radio went silent for a few seconds as if the dispatcher was trying to build up his courage before talking to his irate boss.

"Uh, the horse, sir, the horse isn't dead, yet."

"And," asked Tommy Lee, stretching the word into at least three syllables, "what? Would they like me to drop by and shoot it?"

"And the call came from Charlie Hartley. He was quite distraught. Pitiful actually. The vet told him he thought it was poison. Charlie insisted I let you know."

Tommy Lee sighed and the anger left him. He knew as well as I now did how important those horses were to the old man. "Okay," he said. "I'm sorry. See if you can get somebody up there."

"We're spread to the limit, Sheriff. It'll have to be early this evening when the new shift comes in."

I raised my hand and caught Tommy Lee's eye.

Chapter 9

The sun was dropping behind the ridge of Hope Quarry as I drove around Charlie's house to the barnyard. Parked beside the plow was a white pickup truck with Blanchard Large Animal Vet lettered on its side.

I wasn't sure what I was going to do or say in the barn. I wasn't sure why the hell I had volunteered to come up here. Because it was Charlie and I liked him. Because I liked Reverend Pace and the fact that he once buried an old man's dog. I might be at a loss for words, but I could be there.

Charlie Hartley leaned over the stall railing and watched the veterinarian examine Nell. I slipped quietly beside him.

"Tommy Lee sent me," I whispered.

"Thanks," he said and turned his concentration back to the suffering animal. He didn't seem to care that I didn't have a badge or a uniform.

Sporadic convulsions rippled across the mare's flank, and her nostrils flared with every breath. Charlie shuddered with each sign of the animal's agony. All I could do was reach my arm across the old man's shoulders and give a squeeze to say hang on.

Rich Blanchard tucked his stethoscope in his jacket pocket and shook his head. He gave his patient a gentle pat on the rump, then turned to us.

"I'm afraid the foal will be stillborn. We'll deal with induced labor later."

Charlie laid his face against the back of his hands and suppressed a sob. "And Nell?" he managed to ask.

"The next few hours are critical. I've given her a heavy dose of mineral oil and an injection of a general antitoxin. I'm also flying a blood sample to the Veterinary Research Lab at NC State. In the meantime, we'll rig a sling to keep her on her feet. Keep her flushed with large quantities of distilled water. You can get it by the gallon at Ingle's Supermarket."

"You think she was poisoned?" I asked.

"Never seen anything like it. No sign of disease. Yes, I think she ingested something toxic. Charlie said she was fine until yesterday evening."

"Downright frisky when I let her out to the south pasture," confirmed the old man.

"The stallion with her?" asked the young vet.

"No. Keep them separated."

"And he is fine," observed the vet. "Must have been something she got in the pasture."

"Who'd want to poison my Nell? That's why I called the Sheriff."

Blanchard shook his head. "I don't mean to suggest it was intentional. Maybe somebody dumped rancid garbage. Then she ate it, or it got in the water supply."

"Never found any dumping on my land, and the only stream in that pasture flows from the quarry. No way for anybody to get back up there since the road growed over."

"Your other horse been in that field?" I asked.

"Not for a couple days."

Rich Blanchard thought for a few seconds. "I'm going to take a sample of the creek water and send it with the blood. Might be nothing, but right now we got too many questions and no answers."

He pulled a clean vial from his black bag and walked out the back to the south pasture. Then I heard car doors slam in the barnyard. Charlie stood oblivious to the sound, staring at his beloved mare.

"I'll see who's here," I said.

Reverend Pace and a young woman were standing by his maroon Plymouth Duster, circa 1970. He smiled at me and pointed to the veterinarian's truck.

"Is she foaling?"

"No," I said in a tone that dissolved the smile from his face. "The foal's dead. The vet thinks Nell ate something poisonous. Charlie may lose her too."

Reverend Pace leaned against the hood of the car. "Oh, dear God." He squinted his eyes shut as if he wanted the sockets themselves to close up. "Don't let that happen."

He took a few deep breaths, opened his eyes and turned to the woman beside him. "Wait, here. I'd like to speak to Charlie alone."

I took his words to apply to me as well, and I stayed with his companion as the old preacher disappeared into the barn to comfort his friend.

"I'm Barry Clayton."

"Sarah Hollifield. I'm an intern with Reverend Pace. Just started today. We were on our way back to town from another visit, and he said he wanted me to meet someone. Guess we came at a bad time."

"No. You came at a good time. I can't think of anyone who could help Charlie more."

"Is it bad?" She looked to the barn and her smooth forehead wrinkled with concern.

Sarah couldn't have been more than twenty-four or twenty-five. Her reddish-auburn hair framed her cherub face in a simple page-boy cut. She wore a green, V-necked sweater over a crisp, white blouse that was open at the neck and exposed a small gold cross hanging from a delicate chain. Her skirt was a muted tartan plaid hemmed just below the knee. Her black flats, dangerously close to a fresh horse-dropping, were polished to a soft finish. I imagined they had been extracted from terry cloth shoe bags assigned a special compartment in her suitcase. She was the eager angel wardrobed in a parochial school dress code.

"Bad," I said. "About as bad as it can get for the old man."

Sarah lifted her right hand to her mouth and chewed her fingers nervously. I noticed a smear of blood on the cuff of her sweater.

"Did you cut yourself?"

"No," she said absently. Then she saw I was looking at her sleeve. "It was in Reverend Pace's car. Must have been from the rabbits."

"Rabbits?"

"Yes. He said somebody left him rabbits they'd shot. Just dropped them on the front seat." She shook her head in amazement. "He said it happens all the time. People give him vegetables, deer meat, even pigs' feet." Her mouth scrunched up at the thought and she tried to pick off the flecks of dried blood. "Reverend Pace warned me to wear a different outfit next time, and that I especially wouldn't want to step in any surprises in these shoes." She glanced down and saw the pile of horse dung. "Oh, my." She edged closer to me. "And he said this skirt will never make it over a barbed-wire fence. 'You applied for field work, Sarah. That's just what this is.'" She smiled. "He told me when he first started, he rode out in the hills wearing a tailored suit, and then walked home with a load of birdshot in his rear. Learned the hard way never to dress like a Federal Revenuer."

"Where have you been?" I asked.

"This afternoon we took a sugar-cured ham to a family that lost a child."

"The Colemans?"

"Yes."

"But they wouldn't be home," I said. "Reverend Pace should have known they went to Kentucky last night."

"Oh, he knew. He said it would be easier for them to accept the gift if they just found it when they got back. He didn't even leave a note. He said they've got a long row to hoe, and they don't need to worry about thanking a preacher they don't know. I couldn't believe the Colemans didn't lock up, but I guess they don't have anything worth stealing. Reverend Pace just looped a rope around the shank bone, double-knotted it and hung the ham from the woodstove pipe. Then we closed the door and walked around their property looking for rocks."

"Rocks?"

"Yes. Do you think he's kind of eccentric?"

"No. I'd say he has a practical reason for everything he does." I also knew if Pace and his intern had been on visitations all day he hadn't heard about Fats McCauley. I'd catch him alone before I left. I walked over to his car and looked in the front window. "Did he leave the Colemans the rabbits too?"

"No. He took them out before he picked me up. He said greeting me with a couple of dead bunnies would be too much." Her brown eyes widened at the thought. "This is a lot different than seminary, Mr. Clayton."

"They both sound like they're from another era," said Susan. She lay stretched out across the braided throw-rug on my living room floor. Beside her, George nibbled a leaf of lettuce while Susan scratched the guinea pig behind her ears.

George had been my transition from married life to single life. Not that I believed a wife could be replaced by a rodent, although I know some divorced men would argue that point. Some zoologists argue a guinea pig is not a rodent. I did not mean to insult wives or guinea pigs. I had just wanted someone to come home to.

The pet store owner had assured me of the animal's masculinity, and my new companion had been thereby dubbed Curious George in honor of the playful monkey whose adventures I had enjoyed reading as a child. Within the first

My Jeep lurched forward as the truck rammed my rear bumper.

"He's trying to wreck us," yelled Taylor. The panic in his voice told me he was as scared as I was.

We raced on. I pulled my left arm away from my body, ignoring the shoulder pain and gripping the steering wheel as tightly as I could. The truck bumped us again, and then swerved into the other lane.

"Oh, God, his passenger window's down," said Taylor. "He's gonna shoot us!"

I pushed the Jeep to sixty-five. A sign blurred past. One-lane bridge ahead. I moved to the center, crowding the pickup over. I knew the road bottomed out at the creek and then ascended again. The bridge was upon us. The truck swung against the side of my vehicle, but the Jeep held the road. We shot through the single lane bridge as one, missing either railing by inches.

If the pickup didn't wreck us, the speed would. I knew I could never make it through the hairpin climb ahead. I had to get the truck off my tail or be rammed into the mountain. That meant risking a few seconds with it alongside. I eased up on the gas and braced myself, ready to brake as soon as the rear was clear. Then I would be on his tail. "Hold on," I shouted to Taylor.

The truck came up beside us. I expected the driver to try and run me off the road. I risked a quick glance and saw the shadowy profile of Leroy Jackson illuminated by the dashboard lights. He turned toward me and lifted a shotgun with his right hand. I slammed on the brakes a split-second before the muzzle flashed. The Jeep's windshield exploded.

Jackson's pickup rocketed ahead as the Jeep's tires squealed against the pavement. I was thrown against the steering wheel. Rain and wind blasted in, snatching my breath away. The Jeep fishtailed off the edge of the road, and careened out of control. I saw the bent and broken shapes of dead corn stalks fly up in front of us as we tore across a muddy field. A grass embankment caught the left front wheel, catapulting us into the air in a spiraling roll that flipped heaven and earth and sent us crashing upside down in a mix of mud and weeds. My head smashed against the door beam and my left knee jammed against the steering column. I nearly passed out from the pain.

I managed to undo the seatbelt and tumble down to the crumpled roof. Taylor was either dead or unconscious, hanging from his seatbelt beside me. I had to get out. Leroy Jackson would be turning around and heading back. I had only a moment at best. I felt for my pistol but it was gone. Everything inside was scattered. I reached out farther and my hand touched a string. Josh's bow had been hurled from the back to the dashboard. The quiver was attached and a few arrows were still clipped in place.

I struggled through the hole in the windshield, dragging the bow and arrows with me. Crawling through the mud under the Jeep's hood, I avoided the headlights. I wished I had turned them off, but it was too late now. The twin beams angled into the sky, and through the sheets of rain, I could see a cross on a steeple. We had crashed beside Hickory Nut Falls Methodist Church. Maybe a phone was inside and a place to hide.

I got to my feet and my left leg buckled under me. The knee throbbed. The bow became a crutch as I limped up the hill toward the rear of the church, staying clear of the Jeep's lights. I kept wiping my eyes, not from the rain but from the warm blood that trickled down my forehead. I didn't know how deep the gash was. It was the least of my worries.

The congregational cemetery lay between me and the building. I tried to find a row of headstones to use as a guide for an aisle of open ground. Stumbling across a grave marker in the dark would not only be painful, it would also be fatal if I couldn't get back up. I had about fifty feet to go when I saw the single headlight come down the road. Jackson drove past the entrance to the church, stopped, and backed up. I dropped behind a double-grave monument as his headlight raked across the parking lot and swept the tombstones. The chill of the falling rain did not compare to the cold fear welling up inside my stomach. Fate had dealt a cruel hand. I was back in a cemetery facing a shotgun.

Leroy Jackson parked his truck at the edge of the lot where there were no grave plots between him and the wrecked Jeep. I watched lights and shadows flicker through the rain as he used a flashlight to maneuver down the short slope. I started crawling from stone to stone away from him, peering back as I dared to see whether he was coming after me.

I heard him call to Taylor a few times. Then he banged on the side of the upside-down door. There was no answer. He turned his light into the dead cornfield behind the Jeep. I saw the shadowy blur of something moving along the ground. Jackson saw it too. It must have been a possum scurrying for the safety of Hickory Nut Creek at the other side of the field.

Jackson yelled out. "Clayton. Come here. We got to get Odell to the hospital. He's bad hurt. I got no quarrel with you, Clayton." He took a few more steps toward the creek. "I never meant to sic Dallas Willard on you. That was his own doings. Come on, boy. Use your head."

Again, there was movement in the corn. He raised the shotgun and fired. Then he charged forward, firing again. The dead stalks burst apart as if an invisible thresher cut a swath of destruction.

With the blasts still echoing in my ears, I struggled through the graves to the church. I found a back door and turned the knob. Locked. I ran my hand along the edge. There was no deadbolt. I threw myself against it and the old wood jamb splintered so easily I fell inside. I hoped Leroy Jackson was too busy shooting shadows to hear me.

The room was dark and narrow. I closed the damaged door behind me and hoped to find another room where I could lock myself in. If I could just hide for a little while, surely someone would drive by, see the accident, and call for help. Jackson would have to flee.

I felt a rack of robes hanging along one wall. That was probably where the choir changed. I found a second door and opened it. The machinegun sound of rain on the tin roof increased as I stepped into the sanctuary. Dim shapes of pews were in front of me. The main chancel was beside me, bordered by the wall of the choir room. Perhaps there was another room framing the other side, one that had no outside rear entrance and could be locked. The pain in my left leg made walking excruciating. I found a door on the other side of the chancel but it was locked. Dead bolted. The solid oak panels wouldn't yield to my feeble efforts.

A light flashed in the windows of the twin front doors. I heard the latch rattle as Jackson tried to force them open. "Please, God," I prayed. "Let them hold." The sound stopped. He would be going around to the back now. I could only hope to get out the front while Jackson followed my trail to the rear. I made it to the last row of pews when he fired at the front doors. Wood and glass erupted into the sanctuary. I fell to the floor along the side of the center aisle. I clutched the bow in my left hand and drew the string. The pain in my shoulder caused my arm to collapse.

The shattered doors rattled again. The latch still held. I dragged myself halfway under the pew and pressed my right foot against the bow grip. I nocked an arrow. I would aim for his chest. One chance.

The shotgun roared again. Debris rained down on me. Jackson kicked in the doors, and stood on the threshold. He held the flashlight in one hand and a shotgun in the other. "Clayton! Are you in here? Let's make this easy."

Lying on my back with the bow horizontal to the floor, I clutched the string and stretched out my right leg, pushing the bow away from me. The initial pull of the draw was almost more than I could bear, but then I reached the break point and the bow pulleys kicked in, reducing the strain. I silhouetted my foot against the figure in the doorway.

"Come on out. I found your gun in the Jeep. You don't think I'd shoot an unarmed man, do you?" He gave a heartless, soulless laugh that echoed through the sanctuary.

Spine. I remembered Josh talking about spine and the arrow's flight. His bow matched his arrow, a simple target arrow without the razor-sharp broadhead blades that could penetrate the tough hide of a deer. With one arm, one leg, and a blunt arrow, I faced a killer.

Leroy Jackson took two steps inside. I arced my leg a few degrees, keeping my toe lined with his chest. I furiously tried to blink the blood from my eyes. He swept the light around the sanctuary, expecting to find me near the altar, the spot farthest away from him. Suddenly, the beam dropped full on me. I saw the light glint off the shotgun, and I let go.

For one sickening instant, I felt the bow twist against the bottom of my shoe, throwing the arrow higher. I flinched but there was no flash from the gun. Instead, a shower of sparks burst from the wall in a blue blaze that exploded like a Roman candle. The flashlight tumbled from Jackson's hand, flipping backwards to rest with its beam turned squarely upon his face. The eyes were wide and his cheeks and jaw twitched wildly as his whole body jumped and jerked like some electrified marionette. I saw the feathers on the arrow melting. It had struck under his shoulder blade and impaled him like a beetle against the main power cable running along the church's wall. The current, intercepted by the aluminum conductor, diverted through his rain-soaked body.

The smell of burning hair and flesh grew suffocating; then with a loud pop, it was finished. I had just witnessed an execution by electrocution.

Leroy Jackson hung from the wall, well beyond society's retribution. I crawled toward the flashlight, grasped it, and passed out.

Chapter 21

"Jesus, man. What are you going for? The Congressional Medal of Honor?"

As the throbbing in my head lessened, I realized I was back in the same hospital room I'd occupied a few weeks before. Tommy Lee Wadkins was leaning over me. His eye was studying me carefully.

I tried to move and found my left arm again strapped to my side. My left knee was elevated and a bandage encased the top of my head.

"You know what happened?" I asked, my voice cracking.

"Got a pretty good idea. You turned Leroy Jackson into a shish-kabob. Odell Taylor filled in some details."

"I was scared to death, Tommy Lee."

"No, you were scared to die. So, you kept thinking and you took action. I just never would have figured you for Robin Hood. Given the condition you were in, I'm not quite sure how you pulled it off."

"Neither am I. Is Taylor all right?"

"Yes, concussion and multiple bruises. You tossed him around like socks in a dryer. He's in the next room under guard and under arrest. By the way, do you get a discount for booking this same room?" He held a cup of water to my lips and let me take a few swallows. Then he pulled up the chair, turned it backwards and sat down like the day his investigation started.

I looked around. My head was still spinning. The clock read ten-thirty. "What day is it?"

"Only Thursday morning," he said. "Last night a passing car saw the Jeep wrecked in the field by the church. Reece relayed the call and I got there a few minutes after the ambulance. Taylor was conscious but still cuffed and hung up in the seatbelt. He was scared to death Jackson was coming back for him. Didn't calm down till he heard his brother was dead."

"Is he talking?"

"Oh, yeah. He wants to deal except there's nobody left to sell out. Only thing he'll admit to is dumping the waste. He knows he's liable for Jimmy Coleman's death but insists Leroy Jackson pressured all of them and he's no more guilty than the parents."

"What about Dallas Willard?"

"Like we figured, it was all about the land. Pryor was afraid the Willards would sell to Waylon Hestor. He told Taylor to speak to Dallas. He figured a local man was a better approach than some slick Charlotte lawyer. Leroy Jackson was in it the whole time too. He told Dallas he spoke for God's will. Jackson mixed truth and fiction to fuel Dallas' paranoia about the migrants overrunning the land if it were sold to the wrong people."

"But Dallas couldn't stop his brother and sister from doing whatever they wanted."

"Pryor didn't learn about the voting control of the estate until Taylor approached Lee and Norma Jean right after Martha died. They preferred to sell to Waylon Hestor, which meant Pryor and New Shores would have been out on a financial limb. That started the chain of events, and Leroy Jackson pushed Dallas over the edge. Taylor said part of the time between Martha's death and the funeral, Dallas stayed with Jackson. Luke Coleman has confirmed he saw them together. God knows what the bastard told Dallas to keep him in a frenzy."

There was a knock at the door and a nurse stuck her head in. "Time for his pain medicine," she said.

I waved her off. "Give us a few minutes," I said. I ached all over, but I wanted to understand everything Tommy Lee was telling me. "Go on," I told him.

"So, in a way, even the graveyard shooting started with Jackson. Then he hid Dallas with him. Dallas' truck had been parked in a ravine near the compound where it wouldn't be visible from the air. When Pryor learned about it, he told Jackson that Dallas was too much of a liability. He could bring them all down. So, Jackson decided to get rid of Dallas the same night they dumped the chemical waste. Luke Coleman drove Jackson's pickup to Broad Creek, and Jackson rode with Dallas to the spot by the rail bed where we found the truck. Taylor said when his brother flagged them down on the tracks that Thursday night, he had already killed Dallas. Taylor swears he never knew Pryor and Jackson planned to murder him."

"Of course, what else is he going to say if he wants to save his skin?"

"Yeah," agreed Tommy Lee. "Jackson kept Dallas' gun and long coat as souvenirs. I found the shotgun by Jackson's body. Dallas' initials are carved on the stock. Jackson was wearing the long coat, but the arrow hole and burn marks will hurt the resale value."

"You're too much," I croaked. "How about selling me some more water?"

Tommy Lee got up and gave me a second drink.

When my throat cleared, I asked, "And Fats?"

"Leroy Jackson thought Fats had figured out the phony snake story. Barry, I think he just enjoyed killing. A self-proclaimed man of God who played God. Perfect cover for a psychopath. Didn't need much excuse, just opportunity. The Colemans said he got to Kentucky several hours behind them. Enough time to have murdered Fats, and using Dallas' gun gave him the perfect fall guy for the crime. I suspect he saw your name and the word weather written on that note and took it. He might have been watching you for any sign you could cause trouble."

"What about Pryor and New Shores?"

Kyle Murphy discovered the LLC is made up of insiders in the power company. Not Ralph Ludden but some lieutenants looking to make a killing. Like that deal at Enron where assets got placed in outside firms controlled by executives. Greed, plain and simple. The shit is going to hit the Ridgemont electric fan for sure. It will be a PR nightmare in these parts."

"The profiteers try to screw the mountaineers again," I said. "What about the money Fred Pryor withdrew?"

"Bob Cain had arranged for the crew to have free access that night to the construction site including the locomotive. Pryor paid everybody off in cash. He had made it clear he wanted Dallas taken care of but he knew nothing about Dallas being dumped in Hope Quarry along with the waste. Neither did Cain. When the body was discovered and we told Pryor, he made another cash withdrawal and paid Jackson and Taylor a bonus to make sure everyone's mouth kept shut."

"Cain is dirty then?"

"Yeah. But that's an EPA jurisdictional prosecution. I don't care about that ex-candidate."

"Ex-candidate?"

"Cain dropped out of the race this morning." Tommy Lee smiled. "Guess he's not entirely stupid."

"No loose ends then?"

"Oh, there's stuff that will be filled in. I expect the paint on the power pole will match either Odell Taylor's or Leroy Jackson's vehicle. But other than Taylor, we don't have many culprits left alive."

"You know, it's funny about Fred Pryor."

Tommy Lee looked away from me. "Why would you say that?"

"Like you told Taylor last night, it would have come down to his word versus Pryor's. The paper trail ties Pryor to the land scheme but not to the murders he caused. Jackson probably did what a judge and jury could not have done."

Tommy Lee made no comment. He simply paced the hospital room. Somewhere in the fog passing for my brain a light clicked on.

"Wait a minute," I said. "If Leroy Jackson shot Pryor, how did he get on my trail so quickly? Tommy Lee, I think he came from behind the barn where we had been earlier. He couldn't have made it from Broad Creek to there in less than five minutes. He was probably coming to Taylor's. They had to meet somewhere before they went after Talmadge. He saw the patrol car and ducked behind the barn. He saw you put Taylor in my Jeep."

"Sometimes an investigator can be too smart," said Tommy Lee.

"Leroy Jackson didn't kill Fred Pryor, did he?"

My friend stared out the window at the overcast sky. I understood he was struggling with something, and waited while he worked it out.

Finally he said, "Next Tuesday this county will re-elect me sheriff. They trust me to uphold the law, to protect law-abiding citizens. And this county is blessed with law-abiding citizens," he added. "What should a lifetime of obeying the law earn you?"

"Respect," I said. "And maybe a little grace from the powers that be."

"I can get the D.A. to accept Leroy Jackson as the murderer of Fred Pryor. Leroy Jackson had the motive to keep Pryor quiet. We have proof that Leroy Jackson was a repeat killer, and we have a fried Leroy Jackson in the morgue, unable to mount much of a defense. In fact, the D.A. is pressing me for my report so that he can sign off everything from the past two weeks. He's up for re-election too. All those murders will be buried with Leroy Jackson and no one is thinking of looking any further."

"But," I said.

"But you and I know we have some problems. Not only with the timeframe, but with other details as well. Fred Pryor was killed with double-aught buckshot and Jackson used number one. The pump shotgun always left a shell, and yet none was found at Pryor's murder scene. I went up to the Hickory Falls Methodist Church early this morning. Pace and I picked up pieces of the door, pieces embedded with number one buckshot. Number one shells were littered all over the place. Why would Jackson kill Pryor with double-aught and then revert back fifteen minutes later to number one?"

I felt the knot re-tying in my stomach. Tommy Lee's speech about law-abiding citizens was leading in a direction I didn't think I wanted to go. "And you know something else, don't you?"

"Yeah. I noticed one thing at Pryor's murder scene before the rain washed everything away."

"What's that?" I asked.

"Manure. Someone had scraped manure off on the steps to the trailer. Probably what would be caught between boot heel and sole and not come off even after walking, say, several miles into Broad Creek on a railroad track."

"Manure," I repeated.

"Yeah. I took a sample, but I haven't sent it to the lab. I'll wager Tuesday's election that it's horse manure."

In an instant, I understood why Tommy Lee was so upset. A lifelong, law-abiding citizen had seen his family destroyed by a faceless institution. No one spoke for him; no one came to a funeral; no one offered justice. Charlie Hartley had found the killer of his mare and unborn foal. He had made the connection between drums of Pisgah Paper Mill waste and Ridgemont Power and Electric's Broad Creek Project. He had put a face on the guilty institution. The face of Fred Pryor. The man who had sent him a check. I heard Pryor's sarcastic voice in my head. "How many cans of dog food?"

Tommy Lee must have read my thoughts from the expression on my face. "Yes," he said softly. "I can imagine that he politely wiped his feet before knocking on the trailer door. And Pryor came out like he did with us that first day. Wouldn't even let him in. No telling what Pryor said, but I'm sure it was insulting and cruel. The million-dollar wheeler-dealer who couldn't understand what other people value."

"How can you prove it?" I asked.

"Easy," said Tommy Lee. "And that's the damn problem. All I have to do is ask him. He'll tell me the truth."

I wanted to say then never ask. For once in your life, turn your blind eye to a crime and let an old man live out his days.

"I'm an undertaker," I said, "not a law officer anymore. And I'm certainly not a judge."

"I'm not asking you to be either."

I nodded. "However, I am your friend."

There was a knock at the door.

"Come in," said Tommy Lee.

Susan stepped into the room. "How's the patient?"

"Better, now that you're here," said Tommy Lee. He reached down and gave my right hand a firm squeeze. "Thanks for everything. Take care of yourself." On his way out, he said to Susan, "And you, remember this man is in a weakened condition. Don't take advantage of him. This hospital has rules of conduct."

She eased into the chair and took my hand. For a few seconds, we didn't say anything. Tears started flowing down her cheeks.

"Oh, Barry," she whispered. "When I heard the news last night, I thought I'd lost you."

"So, how am I doing, doctor?" I asked.

"O'Malley did the surgery. You've now got a nice set of stitches in your head that match your shoulder. There were torn ligaments in the knee that will require a couple months of physical therapy. We might let you out Saturday." She forced a smile. "O'Malley wants to know if you'd rather just keep us on retainer."

"And you? What are you going to do now that I've broken another Friday night date?"

"I've got to take care of an injured friend's guinea pig, but I'll be here tonight and tomorrow night, and I know when the nurses make their rounds." She leaned over and kissed my forehead.

I reached up and gently cupped her cheek, guiding her lips to mine.

Chapter 22

The November sky spanned the ridges, cloudless and crystal blue. The air was crisp and pure. The bright colors of the tree-covered hills had peaked and descended into muted browns. On the shadowed side of the barn, the chill of the late afternoon gathered force. I stepped with my crutch into a patch of fading sunlight and glanced back into the stalls. Ned whinnied once. I heard the voices of Tommy Lee and Charlie Hartley rise and fall on the autumn breeze, but the words were swallowed in the whispered rustling of dying leaves.

My head started throbbing and I pulled a bottle of aspirin out of my jacket pocket. I choked down two pills without water and watched the last rays of sun disappear behind Hope Quarry. Reverend Pace had been right. As beautiful as the scenery was, it was the people who mattered. The people Pace served, the people Tommy Lee protected, the people my grandfather and father consoled during life's saddest moments, the people who now looked to me to carry on the tradition my father no longer remembered. And because he could not remember, I would not forget.

"You ready?" growled Tommy Lee.

I turned around to find him only a few yards behind me. Charlie was nowhere to be seen. "Are we going to have company?" I asked.

"No. Charlie is leading Ned out to fresh feed."

"What did he say?"

"He said he misses his horse. He asked me to tell you good-bye and he'd be happy for you to drop by sometime."

"Then the case is still open?"

Tommy Lee kept walking toward the patrol car. "No, Barry. The case is closed. Fred Pryor was killed by Leroy Jackson."

I didn't say anything, just limped silently beside him. He stopped at the trunk, turned around and leaned against it.

"That's what the media is claiming," he said. "That's what everybody in the county believes. And who can say justice hasn't been served?"

To receive a free catalog of other Poisoned Pen Press titles, please contact us in one of the following ways:

Phone: 1-800-421-3976
Facsimile: 1-480-949-1707
Email: info@poisonedpenpress.com
Website: www.poisonedpenpress.com

Poisoned Pen Press
6962 E. First Ave. Ste 103
Scottsdale, AZ 85251